Cover illustration: Paper Boat Books

Published by:

Fledgling Press Ltd.
1 Milton Rd West
Edinburgh
EH15 1LA

www.fledglingpress.co.uk

ISBN 9781912280285

Printed and bound by:

Print on Demand Worldwide, Peterborough

This book is dedicated to all those who are far from home.

ACKNOWLEDGEMENTS

This book is inspired by the tragic events of recent years which we have all witnessed – the fate of refugees forced to cross an ocean at grave risk to life, to escape danger and persecution. Although all of the characters in this book are fictional, I owe a huge debt of gratitude to those young people in Scotland whose stories have inspired me to write about Hani, the young Syrian refugee.

I also owe a debt of gratitude to John Buchan's inspiration novel, *THE THIRTY-NINE STEPS*, which thrilled me when I read it at school, as I loved the idea of a mad chase across the wilds of Scotland with a dangerous enemy in pursuit.

A huge thank you again to Clare Cain at Fledgling Press for her patience and continual support, to Yvonne Gilbert for the brilliant artwork and book cover design: to friends and family who are always so encouraging and supportive, in particular my children, Micah and Martha, and my husband Joe. Also my sister, Liz Kumar, and brother, Nick Gollaglee.

But my main inspiration for the characters in this novel has to be – without a doubt – the children and young people I have worked with throughout Falkirk and Stirling, who shall remain nameless, but whose struggles and courage in the face of massive obstacles, taught me so much. This book is dedicated to them.

HANI

It was early morning and a freezing cold dawn stretched across the fields. Twelve-year-old Hani stood in the semi-dark of an immense shed, miserable, cold, tired. He was always tired, couldn't remember a time when he hadn't felt exhausted.

The gang-master's voice invaded his dreams. "Hey! You!"

He pointed at Hani and gestured at the place where Hani was to stand. He knew the routine.

"Come on," his sister Reena whispered at his side.

Reena always made sure that Hani stayed close. It was their one security; they had each other. They would always have each other.

The interior of the shed was like a cathedral or mosque: echoing, dim, full of shadows. But what went on here was neither holy nor religious.

Reena tried to engineer it so that they were near the opening of the shed, which was shaped like an airplane hangar. "If we're near the front at least we can see daylight," she said.

The other option was to head for the shadows at the back, where you could remain hidden, unseen. There was an advantage in that, but Reena and Hani opted always

1

for the light. Not that there was much of it this early in the morning. Hani was almost sleeping on his feet.

They took their places side by side at a great long bench which stretched the entire length of the structure, along with the other workers: hundreds of them, anonymous and sad, robbed of hope, barely speaking.

Looming above Hani, behind wooden slats, was an enormous mountain of carrots reaching as high as the ceiling. He pulled a few of them towards him and there was a faint rumble as more filled their place, "a bit like us really," Hani thought.

He took a carrot in each fist and slid it over the blade set in the bench before him.

One, Two.

But it was cold this morning and the carrots were frozen to the core, so it was hard to top them properly.

He tried again, roughly, and – once he was satisfied – threw the two topped carrots into the carton at his feet. Hani knew that in the past, agricultural workers here were paid by quantity, so it was important to keep up the speed. The faster you worked, the more you were paid. One of the old timers had told him that. But Hani and his sister and the other refugees were fast at their work for other reasons. They were not paid at all – except in food and shelter, and knowing they were 'protected'. A strange bargain of sorts.

When Uncle Giorgio first turned up at the camp, smiling, strolling between the tents, Hani and Reena thought he was their guardian angel. He promised to help them and the other young people he selected. "You are fit and strong," he said. "You will be able to work."

He was their passport out of the Calais jungle, away from the mud and the sad rows of tents sagging in the November gloom. Winter was upon them and Reena and Hani knew that it was only going to get worse, much colder, wetter, muddier, without proper food or shelter.

He promised he would help them and they believed him because they had no choice. There was no one else they could trust.

Uncle Giorgio was not his real name, but he liked the paternal touch, the hint of Italian grandeur. He thought it made him sound interesting, and he didn't really want people to know his real name. There was in fact nothing Italian about him at all – in spite of his name. He was suave-looking, polished, gleaming, as if he had benefited from all the advantages of a good education and a healthy diet. He was an 'entrepreneur', he told the children.

"That is a good word. You will learn about it one day."

"What does it mean?" Hani whispered.

"It means he is a businessman, I think," Reena whispered back.

"Why are we whispering?" Hani asked.

Reena shrugged. She did not know why, but it seemed like a good idea.

"You will have no worries," he told them. "You will be looked after, fed, and as long as you work, you will be happy."

Hani nodded, but he recognized a certain doubtful look in Reena's eyes. His sister wasn't completely sure, he could tell, but it was easier to believe than to question. It was simpler and no one else was offering them any help out of their nightmare.

Hani fumbled for two more carrots from the pile and dragged them across the blade. They jagged and caught again. He lifted his eyes and gazed along the line. Hundreds of workers just like him, stretching to left and right, and if he glanced over his shoulder, the other side of the aircraft hangar showed the same thing – another line of people opposite, silently working, subdued, making no light conversation at all. Obedient because they had to be; they had no choice.

He became aware of shouts in the middle of the shed, voices ricocheting against the corrugated metal walls. Yusuf, the gang-master, was angry.

Reena nudged him.

"Keep your head down," she whispered. "Keep working."

Hani turned back to his mountain of carrots, yawning with fatigue, his hands icy and chilblained in the darkness.

He did not even know where they were. Somewhere in Scotland, a place called Dundee – he had heard that word mentioned – with lots of flat fields and glinting polytunnels. Uncle Giorgio had told them in an oily voice that he would look after them, even though they were illegal.

"Illegal?" Reena asked.

"You have no papers. No passport. You do not exist. Technically."

He said it as a kind of warning and they knew it.

After that, he stopped being so paternal with them; he changed. His voice hardened and they stopped believing that he was kind. Uncle Giorgio had left them here, at this agricultural centre, and they rarely saw him after that. Once or twice he would turn up in a gleaming black car and stand talking to Yusuf and some of the other men, then he would drive away again. They never knew where to.

After two hours Hani had filled a carton and carried it to the middle of the shed where the foreman and gangmaster were sorting the topped carrots.

No one even acknowledged him and he slipped back to his place at the bench and began work again.

A cry and a shout from the gang-master. "You!"

Hani turned and pointed at himself.

Yusuf nodded.

"Yes. You!" he shouted.

Hani could feel his sister Reena tensing beside him, watching anxiously for what would happen next.

Yusuf showed Hani the contents of the box. "These are no good."

He selected one and showed it to Hani. It was not properly topped.

"The carrots have ice in them..." Hani began, but Yusuf cuffed him across the back of the head.

Reena, watching this, flinched, and Hani went silent.

Yusuf hurled the carrots back onto the bench in front of him, with the instruction "Do them again!"

An hour later as he was still working, the gang-master stepped forward and checked the blade in front of Hani. It was embedded in the bench itself so that the workers could take one carrot in each fist and drag it across, before dropping the topped carrots in the crate at their feet.

The gang-master pushed Hani aside, and made to sharpen the blade.

When that was done, he pushed Hani back into place.

Reena watched all of this, her heart aching for her little brother whom she had promised to protect.

Hani glanced sideways at her and she smiled encouragingly. "Things will get better, Hani," she whispered. "This won't always be our life, I promise you."

Hani smiled back to make her feel better, but he knew she could not promise that. No one could. At the same time, he wanted to protect her, his sister, and felt helpless because he couldn't.

They could try to run, but there were dangerous men who would stop them, and anyway, where would they run to? Who else would give them shelter, food, warmth, such as it was?

They had no choice but to endure.

BLOOD

Hani gazed out of the hangar at the morning light as it began to steam on the distant fields. A sudden pain assaulted him, like a bee sting. He should have been concentrating. The sharpened blade had sliced the flesh of his right hand.

Blood spurted and to his shame he began to feel faint. Reena leapt to help him, but even as he fought the dizziness his legs collapsed from under him, and all he could see was a mountain of carrots growing ever taller and higher.

They made him sit in a corner on the concrete floor and the gang-master stepped towards them.

"You!" Yusuf said, looking at Reena. "Back to work."

Then Yusuf bent down and inspected twelve-year-old Hani. He seemed to speak gently when he said "What will I do with you?" and for a hopeful moment Hani thought he had detected a touch of compassion in the man.

"If you cannot work?"

Yusuf lifted one long finger to his own temple and gestured, as if holding a pistol there. He fired the imaginary pistol then shrugged and laughed.

Hani was terrified.

*

"Hani in Arabic means '*happy, joyful, delighted*,'" Reena had told her little brother, on their journey over here. Hani did not feel like that right now. It was a long time since life had lived up to the expectations of his name.

He had memories of fleeing the bombed-out ruins in Syria, of war-torn streets reduced to rubble, the crump of bombs and missiles, the terrifying balls of red flame, the laser-show of military might sweeping across the city skyline with deadly precision while they sheltered and hid in the ruins like rats, with no electricity or running water. He also had memories of a time before, when they had lived in a beautiful apartment, when he had friends and schoolbooks, and a leafy rooftop garden, when fountains would trickle against ornamental tiles and catch the sunlight, but these memories were becoming harder and harder to retrieve.

Instead, what replaced them were nightmarish visions of crossing the water, the terror of that crossing, seeing others drown. Then arriving in Calais and waiting in interminable queues behind wire, living in mud in the tent city, the Calais jungle, without parents to protect them.

And then Uncle Giorgio, with his smile.

And now this...

Reena and Hani's parents had stayed behind in war-torn Syria. It was hard to imagine they might still be alive. They had paid a great deal of money, all their life's savings, in order to pay a trafficker to take their children across Europe to safety.

They could only afford to pay for Reena and Hani – not for themselves. It was a sad parting and the children tried not to think of it. If their parents had known, would they have parted with their money and their children so readily? They had had no choice.

Once they were loaded onto the inflatable raft which was to transport them through high seas, squashed in with a hundred other people, they never saw the trafficker or their passports again.

Hani closed his eyes. He had a terror of the sea. He could still hear the persistent wailing of a small child, young men clutching the side of the raft, the terror in their eyes as the waves rose and splashed their faces. Grey waves bearing down on them and no land in sight. No food or water and no hope. Reena had clung to him, holding him close. *If we drown, we drown together...*

The terror of that crossing is something that will never leave him; it will never fade, and he will never forget it until his dying day.

When one child fell in the sea, no one could save him – not even his mother's desperate screams. He was left to drown.

They saw another craft, several hundred yards away take on board water, flip and sink. Everyone on board sank and drowned. Hani turned his head and watched the small coloured specks on the surface of the sea that were people, crying, waving their arms. Who could save them? They were quickly swallowed by the height of the waves.

Hani and Reena still do not know how they survived that journey.

And when they got to Europe?

No one was waiting for them there. No one wanted them.

Except Uncle Giorgio.

They were a plague on the face of the planet.

"One day we will write to Mama and Baba," Reena whispered at night, when they lay on their dirty mattress. "We will tell them we are safe. Ask them to join us."

"I'd rather go back to Syria," Hani said, thinking of home.

But when he thought of home he thought of a place that no longer existed, that had been bombed out of existence, flattened, scoured, reduced to rubble. They did not really believe their parents had survived in all of that.

Their mother had been an English teacher in Aleppo, their father a doctor who cared for people, worked to heal the sick. The hospital he worked in and the school building their mother taught in had both been destroyed in the fighting. Children wanting to learn, and sick patients unable to move, were seen as easy prey and were deliberately targeted. They had moved from their modern apartment with its beautiful views and balconies to a derelict room in a ruin with no electricity and no running water other than that which ran down the inside of the walls when it rained. They had once led lives like the people in Europe, with modern conveniences and luxuries, surrounded by the chattering of TVs and radios, laptops, the internet, washing machines... but once the war happened they lived in darkness, sitting in the circle of one candle, which hid the filthy broken walls from view.

Hani's mother had cried a lot. He remembered that... but he did not want to think of it because she had always been so strong before the war.

Reena suddenly appeared next to him in the shadows, smiling, and handed him something.

A chocolate biscuit in a gleaming silver wrapper. A bright treasure.

"Where did you get it?" he gasped.

She winked and nudged him. "Come on, stand next to me and work. We don't want the ogre noticing us, or he'll think you're lazy."

"I'm not lazy," Hani said immediately.

"I know you're not," she smiled.

How did Reena always manage to have the most reassuring smile, even in the blackest of times? She would be a teacher one day, like their mother. She could tell stories, and loved reading books.

There were no books here, though.

Reena had thought about teaching the other children, setting up her own school here – wherever 'here' was – but there were not enough hours in the day. They were worked from dawn till darkness fell, and by the end of their shift they were too exhausted to do anything other than collapse on their mattresses.

"Eat it," Reena said, "it will make you feel better. Keep up your blood sugar."

Hani shook his head.

"Share it with me!" But she refused.

"It is for you. I had one earlier," she lied.

He couldn't bear to eat it in front of his sister. "I'll save it for later," he said, slipping the silver-wrapped biscuit in his pocket. "We'll share it then."

Reena held out her hand and pulled him upwards.

Yusuf was watching them from a few yards away, even though he was pretending not to. Reena could feel his eyes on them, so she kept her head down and told Hani to do the same.

They stood at their work-bench, the only place they now knew, and dragged the frozen carrots across the blade, for hour after tedious hour.

Carrot-topping was not the only labour they were given. It changed with the seasons. In summer, they would pick berries and leeks in vast polytunnels.

But for now it was carrot-topping, mountains and mountains of frozen carrots, still rock-hard from last night's frost.

REENA

When Hani woke up he knew something was wrong. Reena was not beside him on the mattress, that's why he felt colder, an icy breeze creeping under his filthy blanket.

He sat up, looked around.

Darkness.

The other workers were still sleeping.

"Reena?" He whispered her name, but there was no reply.

He stumbled to the door and looked out into the yard. He could hear a dog barking, and two men standing at the back of a lorry. They were talking; their voices low and murmuring.

"How many, then?"

"Just the one this time."

"Where…"

"Balnakeil Bay. North coast of Scotland…"

"*Balfour House?*"

"That's the one!"

Hani listened, committed the words to memory. Balnakeil Bay. *Balfour House.*

He stared across the yard, and in a blinding moment of realisation felt sure that his sister Reena was inside the back of that truck. He then did what he knew she would not want him to do – he ran out into the darkness, screaming, crying out.

Yusuf caught him in his arms, and flung him back with a slap to his face.

He lay winded on the ground. "My sister," he wept. "Reena!"

Then there was darkness.

In the midst of that darkness he was vaguely aware of an engine starting up and the truck driving away out of the yard. Without him. And his sister Reena was in the back of that truck, heading for the most northern part of mainland Britain. For what purpose, he did not know. But he clung to those four words he had heard, repeating them over and over so he would not forget.

Balnakeil Bay. *Balfour House.*

The day was supposed to carry on as normal even though his sister had vanished.

He tried to talk to one of the other workers, but no one wanted to know. They had their own miseries to bear.

"They took her in the night, and I don't know where. *Balfour House*? Have you heard of it?"

No one answered him.

No one replied.

The gang-master Yusuf took him aside, and looked calmly at Hani through his hooded eyes. "Hey," he gestured with his head. It was as if he could anticipate what Hani's next move might be. "You run away from here? You try to escape? Your sister, then... she suffer," he drew a fingertip across his own throat to emphasize the point.

Hani said nothing. He had said too much already, and he knew it.

He spent the long day standing at the carrot-topping bench in the giant hangar along with everyone else, taking the carrots in his fists, dragging them across the blade and dropping them into the crate at his feet, wiping away the tears with the back of his sleeve. He stared along the line. The place next to him was empty and at the entrance he could see the morning light creeping steadily over the fields.

Was it really possible that his parents had sacrificed their life savings for this? And was he now condemned to a life of slavery, standing forever in this shed, topping carrots, or in another sweltering hot polytunnel somewhere, picking berries, for fear of any harm coming to his sister? Was that the way it worked?

What would his parents think if they knew? They thought they had sent Reena and Hani off to a life where they might be welcomed and helped, away from the hell-hole that had become Aleppo, where big super powers like Russia and America fought their bitter wars on territory that was not their own, ripping apart Hani's country and his home. His parents had used up all their life savings, in the hope that their children would be rescued from war.

And now here he was, afraid to make a move to rescue his sister in case they inflicted some harm on her. But he could not stay here and continue to live – if it could be called living – without knowing what had happened to Reena.

By mid-afternoon he had come to a decision. *If I am so insignificant to them, then it will not matter if I run away. They will forget me.* He had made up his mind.

He had to find Reena.

MIA

Mia sat at the back of the classroom, trying to be invisible as usual – the new girl who didn't quite fit in. She was small and quiet and shy – on first appearance, that is, but appearances can be deceptive.

Halfway through the history lesson she felt a sharp rap on the side of her head. She pretended not to notice, even though it stung. Someone had fired a missile across the classroom at her.

She sensed rather than heard a ripple of amusement at her expense.

Jamie – a notorious trouble-maker – let out a deliberately protracted yawn as he slouched back in his chair.

Mrs Mackenzie ploughed on, regardless. "However… interestingly enough… something the British have always been very proud of is the fact that they were the very first nation to deplore the slave trade."

"Deplore?" Jamie sneered.

"It means object to, Jamie," Mrs Mackenzie said patiently.

"Didn't know this was an English lesson as well, Miss."

An icy silence fell across the classroom as Mrs

Mackenzie fixed him with a bayonet stare. Jamie leaned back in his chair and stared right back at her.

"A word with you. Outside!" she said quietly.

"What? I haven't done anything, Miss."

"Out! Now!"

One or two of the girls sitting near the front sniggered as he slouched past them between the rows of desks. He winked at them and flashed a thumbs-up.

Mia didn't snigger. She felt sorry for Mrs Mackenzie, trying to teach a bunch of kids who clearly didn't want to be taught.

Jamie pushed the back of Mia's chair on passing, just a subtle reminder that he still had her in his sights. "Later," he whispered beneath his breath, so that no one but Mia heard.

Mia was sure Mrs Mackenzie had noticed the shoving, if not the whispering, but would she do anything? Probably not. The teachers never did.

She had been bullied since the day she arrived at this school six months earlier, and in spite of everything they told her, it was not getting any better.

She bent her head over the page, aware of Mrs Mackenzie moving towards the door. She knew what was coming next: they all knew. The teacher stepped outside to 'have a word' with Jamie.

As soon as she left the classroom the girls at the front turned and whispered, nudging each other. It was the moment Mia always dreaded – an empty classroom with no one in charge.

"Look at little Princess Mia," one of them laughed. "Getting on with her work, as usual."

"Yeah, look at what she's wearing," another sniggered.

"Is that – *actually* – school uniform?"

Mia said nothing and no one leapt to her defence. She was still the new girl.

She stared at the page in front of her, the words dancing before her eyes. If she ignored them, it would all go away. *'It was not until 1833 that an act was passed giving freedom to all slaves in the British Empire.'*

Mrs Mackenzie returned, followed by a smug-looking Jamie who did not look in the least bit chastened.

The teacher's gaze swept the classroom, the rows of desks, lingering the longest on the girls at the front.

"Now, where were we?" she murmured.

"You were saying, Miss," said Chloe sweetly, batting her spider lashes, "that Britain was the first country to abolish slavery."

Mrs Mackenzie brightened. "Excellent, Chloe. So you were listening, after all."

Fifteen minutes later, Mia listened to Mrs Mackenzie's final summing-up before the bell. "It's worth noting at this point," she finished, "that hopefully we live in a much fairer society today and here in Scotland we can be proud of our track record. Slavery is a thing of the past… but why is it still worth studying the topic today?"

She threw the question back at the class, and waited.

No one said anything. They were desperate for the bell to go, so they could exit fast. Eventually Jamie put up his hand.

"Yes?" Mrs Mackenzie sighed.

He waited till he had the attention of the entire class before speaking, then slurred his words very slowly, for maximum effect. "It's not worth studying, miss, but we haven't got a choice, have we?"

Mrs Mackenzie went slightly pink and the girls at the front collapsed into a fit of the giggles.

As the bell rang the whole school exploded, pupils pouring from the exits.

Mia hoisted her bag onto her shoulder and waited for the crush to die down. She was pushed from behind, and laughed at. Jamie, Chloe and their pals threw back their heads and burst out laughing. Then the others went on home, out into the streets.

Mia walked slowly down the long white corridor, slipped inside the disabled toilet on her left and waited. She did this on purpose, so she could avoid walking home through the streets at the same time as everyone else.

She waited until it was quiet then let herself out again.

Stillness, at last.

This was a new building and the teachers said they were lucky to have it. Mia hated it. To her it was like a prison. One side of the corridor was composed of rough white breezeblocks; on the other were long glass windows from floor to ceiling, overlooking a pebbled forecourt which the pupils were not allowed to enter.

She stared at this sad little courtyard now, which boasted a few fake plants, with white and grey pebbles that had been transported from some distant beach and plonked here as a way of trying to 'pretty' the place up a bit. It hadn't worked.

The one or two striplings planted behind wire mesh were dying. A crisp packet blew in the wind. That's why the pupils weren't allowed in there. It was 'to look at' only. *Look, but don't touch.*

She stopped when she got to the big glass doors at the entrance. The secretary and receptionists were still behind their desks. They glanced up, wondering who was still hanging about. Then they saw Mia... ah, no-one of any importance. They glanced down again and began tidying up for the day, clipping bits of paper together, opening and closing files.

She put her head down, pushed through the heavy swing doors and began her own walk home.

'Home' for Mia was a small semi-detached house in the grid of interlocking streets which made up the town of Grangefield. She hadn't always lived here and she could not force herself to like it.

It was a relatively new town on the banks of the Forth. Across the bay was the Kingdom of Fife, which sounded very grand. Mia caught glimpses of it sometimes when she walked near the estuary on lonely Sunday afternoons when there was nothing else to do.

She was fostered by Angie and Clifford, a well-meaning couple who had been fostering young people for years. Mia was just one more in a long string of 'cases' which had passed through their doors, no more or less remarkable and no more cherished than the rest.

She unlocked the front door into the tiny narrow hallway, where a radiator was hanging off the wall. The builders were in, and Angie 'was up to high doh' with it. She was having an extension done, with a view to taking in extra young people.

Angie greeted her with her usual display of professional cheer. Mia smiled and went up the stairs to her own room – except it was not really her own. It wouldn't be long before another young person replaced her and the same books and posters would be there to greet them and make them feel artificially 'at home', unless Angie and Clifford decided to update the posters and books a little by then.

Mia had never felt at home here. She didn't blame anyone and it was no one's fault, just the way things were.

She flung her bag into the corner of the room, and collapsed on the bed. From her pocket, she drew out three small pebbles, a reminder of the family holidays they used to take in the Hebrides when her parents were still alive. One was pure white, like snow or ice, the other a deep green with rich layers of meridian in it, the other was deep red. She twisted them in her palm.

The island...

She often thought about the island as a way of comforting herself. Coll, with its pure white beaches, glistening skies, and trembling fields of machair or wildflowers.

How had she got from *there* to *here*? A place she did not want to be, watched and monitored by social workers, swallowed up by the care system, simply because her parents had died and she had no other living relatives to support her?

She lived with her gran in Linlithgow for a couple of years, but when *she* died the authorities stepped in and took over. They placed Mia in a children's home, but in view of the circumstances were quick to find a place for her with a good foster family – in Grangefield – a place she had never lived before.

"You'll have to adjust," she was told by the social worker, Margaret. "It's in your best interests to try."

Then Margaret smiled, got into her car, and drove back home to her own husband and children, and house and dog, and goldfish too, probably, leaving Mia to face an uncertain future.

Grangefield was not the most attractive town. It sat on the banks of the estuary, dominated by a petrochemical plant which blinked and spat fumes into the sky. It never snowed in Grangefield. The sleet that fell in winter was sodium-yellow, like the streetlights.

"Mia? You up there?" she could hear Angie calling her from downstairs. "Your tea's ready."

She swung her feet off the bed, and made her way downstairs to the chaos and confusion below.

"It makes sense," Clifford was saying, as he spooned beans onto Mia's plate. "You can watch television afterwards if you like," he added as an afterthought.

"It makes sense, Ange," he went on, once he thought Mia was well out of earshot. "We can take in another three at this rate. Might as well. Pays the bills."

DOGS

Hani ran breathlessly across the empty fields, afraid of the torchlight and the barking dogs. He had done it. He had run away from the network of sheds they were made to sleep in.

He had waited until the long shift was over and everyone was lying on their mattresses in the gloom. Then he slid between the shadows of the yard, climbed a wire fence, and bolted it.

He ran, and now that he was running he could never go back. It would be too dangerous.

It was the barking of the dogs that had alerted his captors. Looking back over his shoulder he could see three of the men gathering in the yard, grabbing torches, letting the dogs off their leashes.

The traffickers had paid a lot of money for migrant workers like Hani; they could not afford to let him escape, otherwise they would pay the price. There were men above them who would take their pound of flesh.

Hani turned and ran, as fast as his legs would carry him. Over the fields, into the darkness, on and on. He could see a copse of trees looming up ahead so he flung himself into them, out of the open. Branches snagged at him, slapping his face and chest. He pounded on until he could go no deeper into the undergrowth, then fell to the ground, peering through the enmeshed branches.

The men were making good progress and he recognized Yusuf among them.

What would they do to him when they caught him? He sat absolutely still, his legs and haunches aching. Any slight sound or movement would give away his position.

The dogs...

Hani was terrified of dogs.

Two of the creatures had scattered in the wrong direction, with Yusuf and the men following, but one of them headed his way.

It stopped not feet from where Hani was hidden. It whimpered and sniffed.

He stopped breathing as he waited for the moment when it would open its wide jaws and spring. He remembered what was in his pocket – the biscuit Reena had slipped him the last time they were together. He saw her smiling face again as she handed it to him. He tore the wrapper off, and held it out gingerly.

The dog whined quietly. Hani broke a bit off and held it out. The dog sniffed, reached forward and took it.

"Good boy!" Hani murmured quietly.

He could hear the distant rustling of the searching men a hundred metres away, but no one else had noticed yet.

"Go!" Hani whispered, gesturing with his hand and trying to make the dog leave. "Go!"

The dog just stared at him, so Hani sacrificed the rest of his chocolate biscuit. He flung it in another direction and the dog ran to catch it.

Hani remained very still, listening to the men as they stood in the darkness, running their torchlight over the fields.

He could hear them talking.

"Leave him. He won't get far."

"But if the police pick him up?"

"Then they'll shove him in a detention centre. Either way, no one will care…"

Hani sat crouched in the darkness, hearing those words repeat themselves inside his head "no one will care…"

He must think of Reena. Reena would care. He must look after himself for Reena.

Once Hani was sure the men were far enough away, he leapt up and crashed on through the undergrowth.

Yusuf's head snapped round, his gaze piercing the darkness.

That was all the evidence he needed.

It had been a trick, and the chase was back on.

THE MONSTER

From the window of Mia's room she could see the petrochemical plant glowing in the dark. It breathed fire into the sky; a monster of tubular steel with elephantine towers and a heart of boiling oil. It burned forever and it never stopped. It ate up the oxygen they breathed, and released poison. It took away their air. Occasionally the sirens would go off, and people would lock their windows, but no one really minded. No one really cared.

It was like a dragon's lair and it breathed dragon's fire, morning, noon and night.

Most people tried to forget it was there, but Mia never forgot.

It gives us diseases, she thought, and bears us ill-will. It has many eyes.

At night, and in the early hours of a new dawn in winter, those eyes would peer at her, fiery-red in the Falkirk gloom.

In her head she referred to it as the Monster.

The Monster was always out there, but she wasn't looking at him now.

Grangefield, Mia thought, was ugly and grid-like, set out by town planners like a board game; snakes and ladders. Life was like that, hit and miss. If you hit a square with a ladder on it you climbed upwards, where good stuff awaited; if you hit one with a snake, you were spat out in some backwater where you did not want to be. At the moment Mia felt as if her life was all about snakes and landing on the wrong squares.

Who would live in a town that looked like a board game, unless you were forced to?

There were cherry blossom trees planted along the streets, and they added a splash of colour in the spring; but it didn't last long before the easterly winds ripped the flowers off; then they would lie like muddied pink tissue paper on the pavement, turning grey underfoot.

There was one thing Mia did like about Grangefield though, and that was the sports stadium. It had its own athletics track. She would go there often to train, but you needed a crowd to really spur you on.

In her more hopeful moments Mia dreamed of running in the Olympics one day.

Her phone buzzed beside her, and its screen lit up briefly in the shadows. The sight of it made her heart sink. They could reach her even here, in the privacy of her room. Nowhere was safe from them.

She thought of Mrs Mackenzie's words. *We live in a much fairer society today*!

Do we? Mia thought.

She tried to ignore her phone but it purred once more.

She lay on her bed, listening to Angie and Clifford climbing the stairs, their tread heavy. She heard them switch on the TV in their own room next door.

The walls were paper-thin and voices came through… a journalist reporting on the state of things '*elsewhere*'.

"An international disaster on a scale never before seen since the Second World War…"

Angie clicked buttons and changed channels, and a different voice leaked through the walls now, that of a slightly peevish-sounding woman being interviewed on the street outside her home.

"I don't care what they say. There aren't enough jobs to go round, and that's a fact. We haven't got room for no more foreigners – not till we can look after our own."

"Switch that off Angie," Clifford grunted.

Silence. Then they opted for something a little more bland. A fly-on-the-wall documentary about home improvements, with the volume turned down.

Mia rolled onto her side, and stared at the blue striped wallpaper which to her looked like the bars of a prison cell.

She didn't hate Angie and Clifford, but they were so flat and dull. Angie talked about her new extension all the time, and what a difference it would make, while Clifford did the maths, working out how many more young people they might be able to foster.

Mia had a trick to help her drift off to sleep, and it gave her comfort.

She imagined herself as a bird of prey floating on high above the island of Coll. She would examine the island from this aerial view. If she turned her head sideways she could see her own wing-tips, and the coastline far below, waves crashing against the rocks, so far away you couldn't even hear them murmur, only see their soft white underbellies unfurling. She felt powerful like this, listening to her own hawk-cry. She flew over Coll where her family used to go on holiday when she

29

was little. She saw the white curve of the bay, the sand made up of the fine ground down powder of billions of seashells, the marram grass blowing in the breeze, camp fires on the edge where one or two families set up their tents, and she could see the little white cottage that – as far as she knew – still belonged to her. There it was, waiting, just like always, reminding her of a time long ago when she still had a family. Before her dreams turned to ash.

Before she ended up here.

In Grangefield, within sight of the Monster.

THE STADIUM

Early the next morning Mia was up and out before anyone else was awake. She would rise early, walk through the dark streets under the fizzy orange sodium glare, and enter the waiting arena of the sports stadium.

Empty. Open to the sky. She would feel the emptiness like a dark prayer or a poem. It was spiritual almost; just Mia and the big peaceful space; cathedral-like, poised. It gave her strength for what lay ahead.

She would train for an hour, then shower, put on her school uniform, fling her bag over her shoulder and leave for that place she'd begun to hate. School.

The oil refinery breathed on in the dark, jet flares igniting the sky. To Mia it looked like Hell on earth. She had read a poem in school once about 'dark satanic mills' which the teacher told them was supposed to be describing the Industrial Revolution. Mia had never forgotten those words, and she thought the description fitted the Monster perfectly.

As usual, she tried not to look. Let the Monster do whatever it wanted, glittering and releasing jets of flame into the dawn. Her body felt light as air after her training. It made her feel strong, relaxed, ready to face the bullies.

31

She had an inner core of strength that neither they nor anyone else could destroy.

But how wrong she was.

THE BEST SOUND IN THE WORLD

The school gates loomed ahead of her in the morning gloom. She was early. The pale pink petals of the cherry blossom trees had been torn off the trees, and lay muddied underfoot. It was raining. It always seemed to rain in Grangefield.

Mia stood under the lip of the concrete overhang of the main building, hoping they would open up before any of the pupils started arriving.

No such luck.

She heard a sound behind her. The others had begun to arrive. Jamie had her in his sights again, she could tell.

She found her way to the lockers, and stood looking through her stuff, with the grey steel door open beside her, hiding her from view. As she heard the crowds gradually building behind her, she felt the familiar knot of dread and anxiety in the pit of her stomach.

She checked her timetable.

First lesson was Music. Not good. Too many opportunities to be singled out, what with Mr Hooper being so lax and wearing his brightly coloured waistcoats. If the class weren't sitting in rows, and were allowed to wander about the classroom freely, that's when the danger points occurred.

Mia had become adept at calculating them ahead of the game – always landing on a square with a snake, instead of a ladder. She lived her life in dread of these moments, anticipating them all the time.

As she pulled her schoolbooks into her bag, she became subtly aware of a group building up behind and around her, but she kept her head down.

That was when the steel door of her open locker came crashing into the side of her head. Not enough to concuss her, but a strong dunt to let her know who was boss. The pain rang through her skull.

When she recovered enough to look up, she saw Chloe and her cohort, including Jamie, walking off along the corridor, glancing back over their shoulders, screeching with laughter and pushing each other in triumphant camaraderie. They were a unit, a gang; they had each other, and they had their families.

Mia stared after them.

She had no one.

If she went to her Guidance Teacher, Miss White, and said "*I think I'm being bullied, Miss White*," Miss White would give her a sympathetic smile, and say "*Try to see it from their point of view, Mia. Are you making the effort to fit in? What you have to remember is this, Mia. There are always two sides to every story.*"

Not helpful, and besides which Mia was not the type of person to go 'snitching' about other pupils, even if she did entertain thoughts of revenge against them. That wasn't her style. To be a 'snitch' had its own price, but if she kept it to herself then Miss White would say "*Well, it's up to you Mia. It's your responsibility. If you don't come to us and tell us what's happening, then how can we help you?*"

Either way, she couldn't really win.

She dragged herself along to Registration, and thought about her training in the stadium that morning. Already the benefits were leaking away, the feeling of optimism and hope replaced by the usual dread.

They would always win in the end.

She had no choice. She could not endure this life any longer.

But there was one thing she could do.

She could run. Far away.

She thought of a small white empty cottage, waiting for her on the island. Its walls might be bare, its furniture broken perhaps, but she could make it full of life again. She could drag driftwood and sea coal from the shore, and light a fire. She could scrub the table, and eat her meals there. She could light the old-fashioned paraffin lamp her dad used to keep on the window sill.

She could make it hers again.

No one could stop her.

Let them try.

She could vanish.

She was practically invisible anyway – except to the bullies.

And once she began running, she could run like the wind.

It was time to make a plan.

She lay on her bed, listening to the heavy tread of Angie and Clifford on the stairs, the mutter of their TV set, a talk show, then some mind-numbingly awful shopping channel. Angie loved shopping.

She waited patiently for the house to fall silent around her.

She listened for Clifford's last routine trip to the bathroom: the flush of the toilet, the bang of the lid, *pad pad pad* back to bed.

A final creak of bedsprings. Then silence, soft as an indrawn breath.

She counted to a hundred then slipped out of bed, lifted her mustard-coloured rucksack from its place by the door. It was light as a feather.

She stopped when she heard someone coughing, waited a moment or two then slowly turned the handle of her bedroom door.

The landing lay in darkness; she would have to feel her way by instinct. She need not have worried though. Grangefield was never completely dark. The glow from the oil refinery shed a fizzy orange radiance through the narrow window above the stairs.

She put her hand on the banister, and tiptoed cautiously down, careful to avoid the creaking stair, third from the bottom. She congratulated herself on remembering this then padded softly down the hallway, past a tool set left lying by the builders.

She opened the sitting room door and made her way through the usual clutter. Then slid open the drawer to the bureau where she knew Angie kept her purse.

She tipped out the contents into her hand. Several coins slid together, and in the leather pouch she found some notes. She took them out and put them away in her back pocket.

If they caught her now, they would shout *thief* as loud as they could. All thoughts of her earlier sporting success when she ran for the school team would be completely eclipsed by this. Mia knew that. She understood exactly what she was up against.

The best sound in the world was the click of the front door as she stepped out into darkness.

Mia walked for an hour through the darkness along the grass verges and cutting across fields, until she came to a familiar roundabout she recognized. There was a service station here, a shabby Burger King, and some garages nearby. She had a plan. She would walk along to Falkirk Railway Station in the morning, and travel by train to Oban. From there, she could get the ferry to her island. But first, she needed to find somewhere safe to sleep.

She crawled under a broken garage door, and lay down. To Mia, it seemed as if she had already covered a great deal of ground, but in fact she was still within reach of the Monster. She could no longer see it, but its poisonous breath still mingled with her own, filling the atmosphere with its silent toxins.

She felt frightened and alone, despite her need to escape from Grangefield. It was a joyless life she lived under Angie and Clifford's roof, and nothing could persuade her to return.

She didn't think she would be able to sleep at all, so it was a surprise when she woke to an early grey dawn. Plenty of time to walk along to Falkirk Railway Station, and use Angie's stolen cash to buy a train ticket.

FLIGHT

Around the farm where Hani worked there were nothing but empty fields and long straight roads where he would be discovered by morning.

The truck which had taken his sister was now far away, travelling through the night, but there was another one leaving soon. He could hear its engine rumbling in the grey dawn. He had managed to give Yusuf the slip, by doubling back on his tracks, and hiding in one of the outbuildings in the yard. He still didn't know how he'd managed it.

He observed the lorry through a crack in the door. Men moved forward to load it in the early morning light. If Hani could not escape across the fields, then perhaps he could escape this way instead?

He slipped into the back of the lorry when no one was looking – a quick shadow darting across the yard when their backs were turned. He hid in the darkness and stowed away on board, so that when the driver climbed into the cab and pulled out of the yard, along the bumping country roads, and finally out into faster traffic, Hani went too. He was thrown from side to side, but at a certain point the lorry picked up a steady speed, and he understood they were on a motorway.

He sat hunched on the floor, wedged between large crates, nearer to the driver's cab where he might be able to hear their conversation and furthest away from the big metal doors. He hadn't yet thought about what he might do once they opened the back and found him there, hiding. But it was too late to worry about that now.

Hani dozed for a while, leaning against a crate, his head on his knees. It began to rain. He heard water swishing against the underside of the lorry, and it made him think of the fountain in their courtyard at home, how it splashed the coloured tiles. But then it began to roar as the tyres tore through the waterlogged roads. The men in the cab had to shout to be heard when they spoke.

One of them laughed.

Hani didn't know what the joke was. It seemed strange to him that they could do that. Imagine being able to laugh and joke when you knew you were destroying other people's lives?

He woke after ten minutes, his stomach cramping with hunger, which reminded him he'd eaten almost nothing the day before in his anxiety about Reena. He was used to hunger, but the thirst was harder to bear. Were they heading north or south? He had no idea. There were no windows to look out of.

A radio muttered in the driver's cab and there was a strong smell of diesel. Hani thought of his sister and his heart contracted. If he lost her, he would not be able to carry on. He had to find her.

Misery sat on him like a stone and to his shame he began to cry. He pushed the tears away angrily with the back of his fist. He thought briefly of his parents. Brave boys didn't cry.

To keep himself sane he kept chanting those words he had heard, so he would never forget them. Balnakeil Bay. *Balfour House.* Strange Scottish words, but he remembered how they both began with the syllable Bal. One ended with the number four; the other with a funny-sounding phrase 'nakeil'.

After a while he was aware of the tempo of the lorry changing, slowing, turning at an angle. They had pulled into a roadside garage.

He heard the driver's cab door open and slam shut again; listened fearfully as their footsteps died away.

Then he crept between the crates until he was near the back of the lorry. He tried to pull the sliding metal door up, but it wouldn't budge. It was locked. He would have to wait for them to open it at the end of their journey.

He had no way of knowing where he was. His eyes had grown accustomed to the dim light, and on the floor next to his foot, he noticed a scrap of paper. An envelope, torn open, with nothing inside it. But on the back were some scribbled instructions.

He spread it flat against his knee.

'*Must arrive at BB for pick-up 1500 hours Saturday. The White Star will be waiting.*'

The White Star? What did that mean?

He pushed the envelope into his back pocket. He wondered what was inside the crates and boxes – just vegetables by the look of it – probably topped carrots – although maybe that was a ruse for something more sinister they wanted to transport in future, like his sister for example.

Something rolled under his foot: a half-full bottle of water was swishing about, left there by one of the men loading up. He was in luck. He grabbed it, unscrewed the lid and drank. It was warm and stale-tasting, but he didn't care. He took small sips so that it would last the journey, then he bedded himself down in the gloom, making sure he was well concealed by boxes.

After fifteen minutes, Hani heard voices outside and he hid at the back while they unlocked the metal door and began to lever it upwards. It lifted with a clatter and daylight flooded the darkness.

There was a minute's silence. Hani held his breath.

"Hey, Karl, come over here and look at this…."

Too late, he realised his foot lay exposed. He tucked it in, then heard a burst of laughter. "Well, if it isn't a stowaway?"

Hani recognised the voice as belonging to one of the men who used to stand talking to Yusuf in the yard outside the carrot-topping shed.

He snatched his moment, slipped between the boxes of goods and jumped down onto the hard tarmac.

"Get him," the other shouted.

Hani didn't wait another second. He turned on his heels and tried to flee, but they grabbed at him before he could make his escape.

A STRANGER'S HELP

Hani cried out for help as he struggled to tear himself away. They were hidden by the truck and a belt of trees at the roadside.

Even as he fought he was aware of a small figure across the forecourt, standing still and staring. The figure moved and suddenly a blur of colour shot towards them, screaming at the top of its lungs, before kicking Karl in the shins.

Then, without warning, Hani felt his hand being grabbed while a tiny stranger – not much bigger than himself – shouted "RUN!"

Hani didn't miss a beat but found himself tearing along beside the girl, holding her hand as she pulled him along. One of the men tore after them, while the other hopped in a circle, nursing his injured leg. But Hani's saviour – whoever she was – ran faster than the wind, and she pulled Hani along beside her.

They sat side by side in the darkness, trying not to move.

They were in a lock-up somewhere; an abandoned garage with a broken padlock on the door and rusting objects lying in the shadows.

Hani turned sideways to examine his companion. She was small and skinny with short fair hair and a mustard-coloured rucksack on her back. She turned her head to look at him, and lifted a finger to her lips.

They waited in silence, listening to the sound of their own breathing. Footsteps passed outside, hesitated, then moved on again.

FASTEST FOOD EVER

Mia raised a finger to her lips. Below the rim of the door, they could see a pair of feet moving slowly.

She looked around the filthy darkness of their hiding place. If they were caught here, they would be trapped.

Then she heard it, the sound she had been dreading.

The rumble of the iron shutter as the men rolled it back up to reveal what might be inside.

Grabbing the boy's hand, Mia poised herself and waited to spring.

Before the shutter was fully up, they were off, swirling away from the grasp of Karl and the other man, straight out of the lane and onto the main road.

They burst into the shabby interior of the Burger King on the roundabout, the only place Mia could think to go.

Everyone turned to stare at them, the attendants behind the counter, the teenage boy wiping the floor with a mop, one or two early morning lorry drivers eating breakfast. Acres of polished floor, red plastic tables.

Mia became instantly calm all of a sudden, fished in her pocket and produced some coins, then approached the counter as cool as a cucumber and ordered a burger in a bun.

44

Then she ordered another for her companion.

All the while Hani was gazing at her as if she was mad.

"What are you doing?" he hissed.

She raised her eyebrows as if to say, "Isn't it obvious?"

She sat down at a table with a view of the forecourt, and Hani reluctantly followed her.

One of the men stood a few yards from the glass window, furiously sucking on a cigarette, his eyes fixed on them.

Hani looked terrified.

"They won't follow us in here," she said. "There are people watching."

Hani raised his eyes and looked at her, "You don't know them. They don't care what people think."

When the girl at the counter shouted out their order, Mia rose from the table.

"Where are you going?" he cried, in a panic.

"To get our food. Stay here."

Hani was starving and tore into his food, but kept his eyes on the men outside.

"They're still watching us," he mumbled between mouthfuls.

"It's okay," Mia murmured, watching the ravenous way he ate his food. It shocked her, to see someone so hungry. She had never seen anyone eat like that before. She noticed how thin he was, and neglected-looking.

A member of staff swept the floor tiles between the tables and looked at them dully, already bored by the prospect of the day ahead. No one showed any interest in the two runaways.

There was a subdued atmosphere.

She glanced about the restaurant at the one or two customers: heavyset men with their heads bent over their food, devouring it, showing no interest in the world around them. Could they risk asking one of those men for help? Mia didn't think so.

In a matter of minutes, her life seemed to have taken a turn in a different direction, and here she was, sitting opposite a boy from another world, who appeared to be in even more trouble than herself. It shocked and comforted her at the same time.

"Who are those men?" she asked.

"You don't want to know. Bad men."

"Why are they chasing you?"

"They took my sister. I tried to escape."

He did not know what else to say to explain the terrible ordeals he had been through. How could this stranger – whoever she was – possibly understand?

"My name is Mia, by the way," she said.

Hani looked at her with his sad dark eyes. "Hani."

"Nice," the girl said. "What does it mean?"

He was not used to people asking him this.

"It means," he paused for a moment, '*happy, joyful... delighted.*'"

They both laughed, but it wasn't a happy laugh.

"My sister Reena told me that," he said. "They took her and I'm trying to find her."

Mia looked at him and nodded as if she had just made a decision.

"I'll help you."

"What? Why would you do that?" He stared at her in disbelief, but the girl just shrugged.

"Because."

46

"Because what?"

"Because…" she hesitated. "I'm running away too."

Hani gazed at her in disbelief. "Why would you need to run away?" he asked.

She looked hurt for a moment and a small silence fell.

"Who are you running away from?" he asked.

"Angie and Clifford," she explained. Hani looked at her blankly. "My foster parents." He said nothing, partly because he was not entirely sure he knew what a foster parent was. Surely it was someone who cared for you?

"They watch TV all the time, and they're building an extension," Mia went on.

Hani watched her, eating his food in silence.

"If they have more space they can take in more cases like me," Mia tapped her own chest. "More cash!" She rubbed her finger and thumb together. "I haven't been with them long. They won't miss me," she added. "I've got plans."

Hani had a feeling he might be about to become part of those plans, but it still seemed odd to him that the worst crime they seemed to have committed – according to Mia – was that they watched too much TV and wanted to make their house bigger, neither of which seemed particularly wicked in Hani's book, compared with the kind of cruelty he was up against.

"Where are we?" Hani asked, looking around him.

"You're in Falkirk."

He looked at her blankly.

"Is that north of Dundee?"

Hani had a vague idea that the hidden sheds where he worked were near a place called Dundee.

Mia shook her head. "Dundee is higher up, on the east coast."

"They were supposed to be heading north," Hani muttered anxiously to himself. "To the coast. To a place called Balnakeil Bay. I have to get there. That's where my sister is."

"I'm sorry," Mia said.

"What are we going to do?" Hani whispered, his eyes drawn again to his captors outside.

"I'm thinking of a plan."

Hani stared out of the window, his eyes wide with terror, as Yusuf's friend threw his unfinished roll-up onto the ground and headed towards the door.

"Well, you had better think quick," he said to Mia, watching this over her shoulder, "one of them is coming inside."

SWITCH

"Put your hood up," Mia ordered.

"What?"

"Just do it."

Hani was wearing a distinctive yellow striped jersey, and he pulled his hood up over his head as instructed.

"Go to the restroom. I'll meet you there in one minute."

She glanced at the door where the men loitered. Something was making them wary of public places, that much was certain. Clearly they had something to hide. Both men tensed as they saw Hani, his hood over his head, disappear to the back.

Mia waited, then stood up and followed the sign to the restroom. She pushed the door open and there was Hani standing under the harsh glare of the overhead light, looking lost and frightened.

"Quick," she said. "Swap your hoodie for mine. I don't know why you're wearing this, by the way, if you want to hide," she added. "It makes you stand out a mile," she muttered as she pulled it over her head.

"It's all I have," was his reply.

Dressed in Hani's jersey, Mia pulled the hood up over her own head and shoved her hands in the pockets. They were roughly the same height and build.

49

"You stay here," she ordered, "and count to 200, then slip out when no one's looking. If we get separated meet me at Falkirk Railway Station. Ask someone if you don't know the way."

The boy watched her in silence, wondering if she was going to abandon him.

"Here!"

She held out her small mustard backpack, the only possession she had.

"You'll need this. Otherwise they'll guess I'm not you."

He took it from her. She was trusting him with all she had, a point that was not lost on him.

"What are you going to do?"

"I'm going to lead them away. I can run faster than them. Remember. Falkirk Railway Station," she repeated.

As she left the restroom the men began to saunter confidently into the restaurant, so she pushed her way through a fire exit, and made a dash for it.

As she hoped, the men gave chase and raced round the restaurant to catch up with her, no longer caring who was watching.

Mia inwardly smiled to herself as she sprinted across the forecourt, along the side of the road, away from the roundabout and the motorway towards the town centre, the men in hot pursuit.

For one fleeting second she remembered the stadium where she trained in the mornings, its empty benches waiting for an audience, the adrenalin burn inside her, the delicate hush of those private moments in the peaceful arena. The stadium was truly the only thing she would miss about her old life.

She had wings on her heels, invisible wingtips which spread and gave power to her flight.

She could hear the men pounding and breathing heavily behind her, but she could also hear their despair and defeat as they fell back and began to realise they would never catch her. She kept going until she was sure she'd given Hani enough time.

The road to the city centre was wide. Normally it was thundering with commuter traffic, great lorries heading for the industrial estates, but it was still a little early for that. She took a left into the forecourt of a car showroom and dipped down between parked cars. She waited, listening to their pounding footsteps grow closer.

She saw them look about.

One of them gave a second glance to the parked vehicles where Mia lurked, and began to head towards them.

She froze against the silver bumper of a parked car.

The other shouted him back. She heard his voice carrying clearly on the quiet morning air.

"Come on, we've lost him. We can't leave the lorry. We'll let Yusuf know where we last saw him."

The other raised his arms in despair. "We're in big trouble, man. They paid big money for kids like him. They'll want their pound of flesh and we'll be the ones paying the price."

"Maybe we don't tell Yusuf then?"

"And then what?"

Their voices faded as they walked away and Mia could no longer hear what they were saying.

She breathed a sigh of relief.

THE MUSTARD BACKPACK

Hani sat in the darkness of another abandoned lock-up where he'd found a place to hide. He fumbled with the objects in Mia's backpack. You could tell a lot about a person by what they owned. At the bottom of the bag he heard some delicate ornaments clacking together. He drew them out – not ornaments, but stones. He fingered their smooth contours. They were beautiful, he could imagine them gritty with sand, and they had a nice natural smell.

His thoughts turned to his sister, Reena.

Was it wise to run away? Traffickers had paid a lot of money for migrant workers like himself and Reena. They were goods, property, and their gaolers could not afford to lose any of them, otherwise they would be the ones to suffer. That's what it amounted to.

Would they really hurt Reena in retaliation? The threats that Yusuf made, was always making in order to keep him obedient, were they true?

Then he thought about the strange girl's last words to him before she fled. "Get to Falkirk Railway Station and I'll meet you there."

How would he find it?

He'd spent six months living on a farm in the middle

of nowhere, sleeping on a bare mattress on the floor beside his sister, topping carrots, picking berries, doing whatever seasonal work was required of him, eating the food that was given him to survive.

And before that, the Camp, the tents and the mud, what they called the Calais Jungle. And before that... the horrors of the journey. The waves growing taller and higher as they closed their eyes against the spray and hung on to the edge of their craft, an inflatable with nothing to recommend it but a passage away from violence.

And it seemed that he still had not arrived. And his parents were back in Syria, where everyone wanted to fight until they completely destroyed his country.

Then he turned his thoughts away from this darkness to more immediate problems.

He must focus.

How would he find the railway station? He leant forward in the darkness and crept his way towards the entrance of the garage. He hated being in the dark. It reminded him of the carrot-topping shed.

He could carry on without the girl. He didn't have to meet up with her again. She might just as easily be a liability if she had people after her too.

He looked down at the mustard-coloured backpack and pulled it towards him, clutching onto it like a life-jacket. Mia, she had said her name was.

He pushed his way through the gap in the rusting garage door, and crawled out into the light.

No one about; no sign of his captors.

He put his arms through the straps and shouldered Mia's little bag onto his back. It was light as a feather – all that she owned in the world.

SINGLE TO OBAN

Mia stood at the entrance to Falkirk Railway Station, at the top of the steps, looking out anxiously for her new friend. She kept her hood up. Would she have been reported missing yet? Would Angie have given a description?

She began to feel conspicuous and was fetching one or two glances from commuters. Her furtive, nervous manner wasn't helping.

She checked the time on her phone. Nearly 8.00 am, beginning of rush hour. She looked out for Hani. Perhaps there was only a slim chance she would see him again. He still had her bag with all her stuff. Not that there was much in it, items of sentimental value mostly. She felt sick at the thought, but even sadder at the idea she might not see Hani again.

As her hopes of glimpsing him in the crowd began to fade, she knew she couldn't wait much longer. Angie would have found her empty bed by now and might be in the process of contacting the authorities, ringing people up, trying to find out where she might have gone. Mia couldn't afford to waste any more time.

She went down the steps into the railway station and joined the queue to buy tickets.

The queue was five deep and she pushed her hands into the pockets of the hoodie for comfort. Her fingers encountered the edges of something. She pulled it out into the light – a small creased photograph of a family group, Hani with his parents and an older girl, obviously his sister.

Mia gazed at it, mesmerized by what she saw.

He looked so different in the picture, younger, happier... cleaner.

Memories from a different time, a different place. He too – like Mia – lived in a world he was not familiar with. *What might have been* had been torn away, shredded by the ruthless machine of life until there was nothing left but this... a creased photograph, lost in the pocket of a jersey.

He too had hit the squares with all the snakes on them.

She heard a cough and a loud, "Next, please!"

She looked up in fright. She had reached the front of the queue without realising it. Quickly stuffing the photograph back into her pocket, she leaned forward and spoke through the glass.

"Can I have one ticket to Oban, please?"

"Single or return?"

"Single... under sixteen," she added nervously.

The man glanced at her.

"Travelling with an adult?"

Mia shook her head.

The man did not comment.

"One child, single, travelling alone, to Oban?"

Mia nodded.

"That'll be £18.40 please. You'll need to change in Glasgow."

For a moment Mia froze and thought of her mustard-coloured backpack. Then she remembered. She searched the pockets of her jeans and pulled out the notes stolen from Angie's purse.

She heard the whir of the machine as the ticket was processed, and then he slid it under the glass to her, where she fumbled for it clumsily.

"Next, please."

Hopefully she was already a thing of the past for him, a forgotten moment in the bustle and chaos of his day. Would he recall any of this exchange later, if asked?

Mia turned and looked up into the eyes of the CCTV camera watching her from a corner of the ticket office. She froze for a moment then pushed through the swing doors onto the station platform. Grey faces under a grey sky, severe, glum, some yawning, oppressed by the thought of another working day ahead.

She scanned the crowds briefly.

No sign of Hani.

What did she expect?

He probably hadn't been able to find the station, after all. Should she go out into the streets and look for him, just in case? She glanced at the ticket in her hand. A single to Oban.

But then she would miss her train, and her passport out of here. She wanted to get as far away from here as possible. She wanted to reach the island, a place where she could feel safe.

She made her way over the metal footbridge to the

platform, clutching her train ticket. Her palms were sweaty and already the edges of the orange and yellow ticket were becoming bent and creased. She slipped it away in a side pocket, fearful of losing it. She had lost enough in her life already.

Her footsteps rang against the metal stairs as she crossed the track down to the other platform.

The station clock clicked forward another minute. At the same moment something made her turn around. She glanced behind her. A splash of mustard, someone wearing her own familiar backpack. She spotted Hani on the opposite platform just as the arrival of the train to Glasgow was announced. The train slid between them so that she lost sight of him even while she tried to attract his attention. She put her head down, and clattered up the stairs through the early morning commuters, going against the stream.

He was standing there on the edge of the platform, looking lost. When she tapped him on the shoulder he spun round, fear in his eyes, expecting at any moment to be arrested or accosted by his enemies.

RUINS

Mia looked delighted. "I thought I'd never see you again."

"Why would you think that?" he asked.

"I don't know," she said evasively, not wanting to admit that she thought he might have disappeared with her rucksack. "I thought you'd never find the station, or that your friends might catch up with you."

"They're not my friends."

"I gathered as much. I've bought a train ticket to Oban. You want to come too?"

Hani hesitated.

"I need to find Reena."

"We can do that as well. But we'll have to hurry. The train will be leaving…"

Again he found himself running along beside his new friend, this strange skinny girl who could run like the wind, apparently, and who had only a few more possessions than himself.

They leapt onto the crowded train seconds before the doors hissed shut and made themselves comfortable in a carriage next to the toilets and the bike racks, where there was less chance of being observed too closely.

"You don't have a ticket, so we'll need to keep our eyes peeled for the guard."

"Ladies and gentlemen, we apologize for the delay to this service. The train for Glasgow will leave in 5 minutes."

Why the delay?

Mia became instantly tense and Hani watched her. She had just caught a glimpse of two peaked caps passing the window.

Police, searching for someone on board by the looks of it.

Mia glanced at the vacant sign on the toilet then slipped inside, motioning Hani to follow her. They waited in silence, side by side, listening to other people boarding: voices, the ticket collector passing by, then silence. At last the train began to move off.

Mia held up one hand.

"Me first. Then you."

She pressed the button and the curving door slid open to reveal four seats beside the lavatory, crowded with tired-looking commuters. Hani was pressed up against the far wall of the cubicle, out of sight.

She stepped out, pressed the button again, and waited for the door to wheeze agonizingly shut. It seemed to take an age.

Then she stood in the space between two carriages, waiting for Hani to emerge.

When he did, a couple of ladies in the seats opposite stared at him.

He took no notice.

They moved through the train to the luggage

compartment at the far end, where it was dark and more secluded. Then they sat hunched up together between the suitcases, surrounded by the rattling and swaying of the carriages.

As the houses and overgrown railway embankments slid past the window Mia breathed a sigh of relief.

"Goodbye, Falkirk," she murmured.

They looked at each other in their swapped jerseys and began to laugh. Perhaps it was the relief after all the nerves.

"I feel like a bumblebee," Mia said.

"A bumblebee? What is that?"

"Buzz-buzz," Mia said, and began to flap her foreshortened hands like wings for explanation.

He laughed.

They sat in silence for a while, swaying slightly with the motion of the train.

"Where do you think they've taken your sister?"

A shadow fell across his face and he shrugged.

"I don't know."

He rummaged in the pocket of his jeans and brought out the slip of paper he'd found in the back of the lorry.

"*Must arrive BB for pick-up at 1500 hours Saturday. The White Star will be waiting.*" Mia read the words out loud.

"What do they mean by pick-up? Pick-up what? And what is BB?"

He shrugged. "I think it's a place called Balnakeil Bay. I heard them talking about it. Also, *Balfour House.*"

"I've never heard of them," she whispered.

Was it possible that he would never see his sister again? How did that kind of thing happen in real life?

"This train stops at Glasgow first. That's where most of the commuters will get off. We change then for a train to Oban."

"What is there?"

Mia shrugged.

"The ferry."

Hani's face darkened at the idea of another boat journey.

"We can get to the island from there. Somehow..." she added uncertainly.

"The island?"

"It's the place where my parents were from," Mia said. "They talked about it a lot, and we went there when I was little."

"Where are your parents now?"

Mia gazed out the window.

"They died. In a car accident. Two years ago. I went to live with my gran."

Hani waited.

"Your gran is not nice to live with?" he asked in surprise.

"She died too. Bad luck, eh?" she added, trying to put a brave face on it. She pretended to be matter-of-fact about it. "She was old. And then they put me into care."

Hani creased his forehead. "What is that? Care?"

It was Mia's turn to frown. "It means they stick you in a home, or place you with foster parents, people who get paid to look after you."

"And they are the people who watch TV all the time and build the big extension?"

"And then they move you on again, while they find another child to foster."

They both fell silent for a while, as the rattle of the train threw them from side to side.

"We are both unlucky then," Hani said quietly. They leaned against the window, looking out, hands hidden away in pockets.

"I hated my school," Mia explained. "I got bullied there."

"Must be tough!"

"Sometimes, but I suppose some people have it worse."

After a while he looked a little awkward and said, "It's nice that you want me to come with you to your island but..."

"But what?"

"I need to find my sister. I need to go here, instead." He tapped the bit of paper before putting it back in his pocket.

Mia took this in, trying not to show her disappointment and hurt pride. Of course he was right. Why would he want to come with her to any silly old island, just because it was somewhere she had once felt happy and secure in the past? It might be important to her, but it was nothing to him.

"So," he said carefully, "you remember this island?"

Mia reached for the mustard backpack and fumbled inside it, then pulled out the pebbles to show him. He reached out a finger to stroke them, pretending he had never seen them before.

"I've had these since I was little. They remind me..."

"Of what?"

"It's beautiful there. Very quiet, with huge curving white beaches and soft sand, and there are fields of swaying flowers – the machair they call it – and there are ruins too."

"Ruins?" Hani said, looking anxious. He knew about those. A vision of his destroyed city crept from the corners of his mind, the streets reduced to piles of grey rubble, unrecognizable, every familiar landmark obliterated, and he wondered why anyone would want to visit a place where there were ruins.

"Yes, *beautiful* ruins," Mia went on. "More people used to live there, but they were cleared off the land a hundred or so years ago. My parents told me about it. So now only the ruins remain."

Hani frowned. He was not sure he liked the sound of that.

"So no one lives on this island now?"

Mia laughed.

"Of course they do," she said. "I'll show you. We'll find your sister first. Then we'll all go to the island together."

"How will we find her?"

"I don't know, but we will."

SWITCHING TRAINS

The train picked up speed and lurched from side to side. It was busy, packed with commuters on their way to Queen Street.

Mia thought about the size and breadth of Scotland, and how in all the world they would be able to identify that one place – *Balfour House* – and the bay it sat on, Balnakeil Bay.

"Google it!" she said out loud.

She pulled out her phone and logged onto the wifi while Hani watched. She typed in the words *Balfour House* but nothing came up at first.

Hani was looking nervous and distracted, but Mia didn't notice. She focussed her attention on her smartphone and keyed in the location Balnakeil Bay.

"Bingo," she said, after swiping her screen a few times. "It's on the north-west tip of Scotland, right at the top."

She scrolled about on Google Earth for a while, her curiosity piqued, completely absorbed in the rough landscape and rocky coastline that slid into view beneath her fingertips. Eventually she saw a faded ochre house standing just above the shoreline.

"Maybe that's it," she said.

She nudged Hani and they zoomed in on the image of a bleak stone house standing isolated and remote above a beach. It had many windows, but they were all small and narrow, like a prison. It had no redeeming features, nothing to soften its appearance. It had probably stood there for centuries, confronting the winds and elements that raged off the Atlantic at this most northern tip of mainland Britain.

"Maybe that's where your sister is? It's Wednesday today," Mia said, thinking out loud. "We've got until Saturday to find the place and see whatever it is they're up to."

Hani wasn't listening. He had become distracted by something he'd seen – or thought he'd seen – further down the train.

"What is it?" she asked.

"Nothing." He shook his head. "I just thought... but it can't be."

Mia followed his gaze. The aisle was crowded with commuters travelling to Glasgow, swaying from side to side with the motion of the train, some trying to read newspapers or looking at their phones, others gazing out the window, trying to ignore their uncomfortable surroundings.

Hani's gaze was drawn towards a man in the next carriage with a profile he recognized. There was something about the set of those shoulders, the way the head tilted, the dark hair... but it couldn't be. Surely he was seeing things?

"Yusuf!" he muttered, the blood draining from his face, and he began to feel sick.

"Hani? What is it?" but he was unable to speak.

Yusuf could not have caught up with him so soon. It was just a coincidence. It was just a man who bore a resemblance to him.

"Hani?"

This time he was certain. He glimpsed the man's face. He was pushing his way down the carriage with dogged determination, manoeuvring his way along the crowded aisle between the bodies, glancing from left to right as he went.

Dread took hold of him.

"It's Yusuf," he said quietly.

Mia looked at him blankly for an explanation.

He turned and immediately began to walk in the opposite direction, away from Yusuf. Mia followed him wordlessly, glancing back from time to time. The dark stranger was inspecting the seats either side of him as he forced his way through the crush.

She sensed Hani's terror.

They pressed on, through another carriage, and another one, until they could go no further.

"We're running out of train," she pointed out.

Hani looked desperate.

"Who is he?" she asked.

"His name's Yusuf. The last time I saw him was in the yard outside a carrot-topping shed where we all worked. I don't know how he could have got here so quickly. Or why."

They looked back at the toilets where the engaged sign glowed an angry red. Hani was sweating, his eyes wide with terror, his face chalk-white.

"It's okay," Mia reassured him, but she knew it wasn't okay.

The engaged sign clicked off, a passenger emerged, and the green vacant sign glowed in its place.

Mia pushed him inside.

"You go in there," she said. "I'll keep an eye out."

Hani did as instructed, while she stripped off the yellow hoodie which had belonged to him, and stood leaning against the luggage rack in her dark grey T-shirt. Nondescript, anonymous; she hoped.

Then she waited to see if the dark stranger came this way.

Why would he be following Hani still? What were those men so worried about? That, once escaped, Hani would let the authorities know what they were up to, and why? Was that it? And then it occurred to her, perhaps Hani had more power than he realised. Sometimes knowledge is power, and Hani knew stuff the authorities would not be keen to admit – that people were trafficked in this country like goods, sold like slaves. The traffickers had paid a lot of money for people like Hani and his sister and they would not be pleased to know that one of them had gone missing.

She remembered Mrs Mackenzie's lesson on slavery. A history lesson, as if all that kind of abuse and horror only existed in the distant past, to be picked over and examined like relics. But here was the truth, the hard facts. The illegal trafficking of people had not ended with the Abolition of the Slave Trade. It was still going on here, on the shores of mainland Britain.

Mia watched the corridor, while pretending to inspect her phone. It meant she could keep her eyes down. The secret of being invisible meant not looking up, not letting your gaze meet the eyes of those around you. She could seal herself off in an invisible bubble of faceless anonymity, just another young person staring mindlessly at her phone, not noticing what went on around her.

She was aware of movement to her right, footsteps heading her way. Someone banged into her accidentally, briefly apologized, and moved on.

He was gone.

He had his back to her.

She stared after him – the man who was even now in search of Hani, tracking him down.

She tapped on the toilet door, and Hani pushed the release button. As soon as it was a few inches open, he slid out and followed Mia back the way they had come, in the opposite direction.

They hoped Yusuf would be satisfied that he had done a complete sweep of the train and found no evidence of the fugitive.

The two did not stop, but kept on moving through the commuter crowds, all the way to the other end, as far as they could possibly go.

Suddenly the overhead intercom pinged into life, and a voice announced that the next stop was Queen Street, and that passengers were advised to take all their belongings with them. *As if they needed reminding*!

"Not long now," Mia said, but both of them were as tense as a pair of cats.

"Don't keep glancing over your shoulder like that," she whispered. "It draws attention. Just stare at your feet. Wait for the train to stop."

Hani's fingers clasped the pole next to him, his

knuckles white, and he did his best not to look around, to make himself as still as possible.

The train moved into the mouth of the railway station, swallowed up by a tunnel of darkness. It slowed, screeching, squealing, while bored passengers waited for the moment when they would be released.

Finally it shuddered to a halt, and then there was the tense wait before the doors hissed open. People started glancing up and down the carriage impatiently as they usually did, waiting for the mechanism to swing into action.

"Come on," Mia nudged him gently, and they stepped down onto the long grey platform, busy with commuters. They moved with the rest towards the gates, where guards were waiting to make sure the ticket barriers worked smoothly, and question any passengers without tickets. A whole crowd of people seemed to be standing on the station concourse, staring up at the display boards above – but it felt to Hani and Mia as if the whole crowd were staring at them.

Keeping their heads down they inserted themselves into the surge of people. There was no sign of Yusuf yet.

Then she stood stock still.

"You haven't got a ticket," she remembered.

"Can't we slip through?"

One glance at the barrier told her that Hani would never get through without a ticket, not unless she managed to squeeze him through at the same time as herself, without being noticed.

And there was another thing: the station concourse beyond the barrier seemed to be swarming with police officers.

"Are they looking for *us*?" Hani said.

Then she thought about the CCTV cameras at the station, and how she had glanced up at one of those black cameras before joining the queue to buy her ticket. To Oban. She imagined her own face on the screen, staring up openly, caught in mid-act. Perhaps they had already questioned the member of staff on duty, found out where she was heading.

They were almost at the barrier now. Soon they would have to feed Mia's ticket into the slot, and she would need to ensure that Hani slipped through alongside her before the turnstile caught him in its steel grip and stopped his progress. Then what would happen? A guard would stop him, question him, and the police officers would notice.

She glanced along the platform. It linked up with other platforms, other trains going to different destinations.

She touched Hani's arm, and pulled him sideways with her.

"This way," she whispered.

He followed her soundlessly, taking care not to look behind him for Yusuf.

Glancing at the display screen, Mia saw that the train leaving in four minutes from platform 14 was bound for Inverness.

"That will do. Hurry!"

They didn't need to pass through another barrier: all they had to do was switch platforms, switch trains.

They glanced in all the windows as they hurried along the platform, and found an empty-looking carriage. They slid into seats beside the lavatory again with a complicit nod. Mia fixed her attention on the aisle, looking far down the train for any sign of Yusuf.

BROKEN PROMISES

They were in luck. No guard appeared to check their tickets and it looked as if they had lost Yusuf.

They leaned back in their seats and watched the industrial fringes of Glasgow recede, to be quickly replaced by rolling fields and open countryside.

They had succeeded in giving both the police and Yusuf the slip – for now. Mia allowed herself to relax for the first time in hours, took out her phone, and located the photograph of *Balfour House* again on Google Earth. She zoomed in to examine its bleak façade, a dramatic sky looming behind it, swept with clouds of yellow and grey. Using the touch screen she swivelled round to examine the same view the house overlooked – a wild beach with white sand, black rocks painted over with splashes of slick emerald green, waves curling in to shore. It looked beautiful but stark.

Hani watched her in silence, his brow furrowed.

Could his sister be there, hidden behind those blank prison-like walls?

The two of them were so absorbed in the world behind her smartphone screen that they almost forgot to keep a look-out for the guard.

"You know, your phone," Hani said after a while, "it might be giving away your location?"

71

Mia lifted her head and stared at him. He was right, of course. Why hadn't she thought of it before?

"I didn't really think I was important enough," she said.

"You need to get rid of it," Hani said.

"I wish you'd said that back in Glasgow!"

"I only just thought of it."

Mia gazed wistfully at her smartphone. The thought of parting from it was painful. She would never have another like it. It was her contact with the rest of the world, her passport to quick information, a library of knowledge in her pocket. What would she do without it?

The whole of the train seemed to be hermetically sealed. There were no windows you could open to hurl the thing out onto the tracks. She'd have to wait till they stopped at the next station, wherever that was.

What Mia didn't know was that she had already been reported as a Missing Person. Hani still did not officially exist – despite the fact his name meant '*happy, joyful, delighted*'. No one was looking for him, other than Yusuf and his men.

"They'll say I'm a thief," Mia said, fingering the remaining notes she had stolen from Angie's purse. "They won't expect any better from me. A child in care…"

She was disappointed because she had spent £18.40 of the money on a ticket to Oban, which was now wasted. She only had £40 left. Not much to build a future on.

She glanced across at Hani.

"I found this in the pocket of your hoodie by the way," she said tentatively. "I thought you might want it back."

He took the worn-looking snapshot from her. That smiling family no longer existed, except in his memory. They had been blown apart by war and misfortune. It hurt him to look at it. He ran a thumb over the image, and focussed in particular on the face of his sister.

Mia turned to look out the window, allowing him his moment of privacy.

After a few minutes' silence she murmured, "We'll try and find Reena. I promise."

He didn't reply.

She wondered why she'd made such a promise, when she knew it would be so difficult to keep. It was the kind of promise adults made. "*I promise I won't die...*" knowing full well they could not promise that.

As the train ploughed its way north the hills became darker, still snow-capped, rough with heather, finally giving way to mountain and moorland. The slick Inter-City seemed lost in the midst of it all. Hani leaned his head back against the seat and gazed at little Mia beside him. She was small and fierce and strong and for a long moment he was glad he had found her. He didn't feel quite so alone anymore, although nothing would ever feel right again until he found his sister.

Hani knew about broken promises. There was no point in making any.

"What is this town we are heading to?" he asked.

"Inverness."

"And what will we do when we get there?"

"I don't know yet, but what I do know is, we're heading in the right direction. The North."

Mia rummaged in her pocket and brought out all the notes she could find.

"We've got £40 left."

Hani noticed the way she said 'we' and was touched by it. It seemed a lot of money, but even he knew it would not last long. He was putting Mia at risk by sticking by her side, and he knew that their chances of avoiding capture were not high.

Then he came out with it.

"Perhaps at Inverness we should go our separate ways."

It was a statement, not a question.

Mia was horrified. "You're not serious?"

He didn't answer.

"We have to get to Balnakeil Bay," she said desperately, "We have to find *Balfour House* and your sister."

"No, *you* have to get to your island."

She stared at him.

"You've been really kind, but I can manage on my own from here. We're more noticeable together."

He tried to ignore the look of rejection on her face.

The thought of being alone again, just when she had found a friend who could share what she was going through, was more than Mia could bear just now, but she was doing her best to hide it, out of hurt pride, he supposed.

"I could land you in a lot of trouble," he murmured.

"I don't care," she whispered. "I'm in enough trouble already. I don't want to be on my own," she added.

He nodded and smiled. "Then maybe we stay together – for now at least."

"Exactly," she burst out. "You'd never manage without me. I can translate the complexities of British life for you."

He looked at her blankly while she sat back in her seat, smiling with relief. Having found a companion, another fugitive to share her journey with, she was not about to give him up so easily.

MISSING

Back in Grangefield the phone rang constantly. Angie and Clifford were questioned and interrogated by police after they reported Mia missing, but nothing untoward had been found. The school were informed and when the register was called out, pupils glibly told their teachers that Mia Shanks was no longer at the school. Her disappearance was like a stone dropped into a pool. The ripples soon closed over and perhaps Mia was right when she thought no one really cared.

Angie and Clifford would soon – over the course of time – be matched up with another young person. As Mia had guessed, they would not bother to update any of the books and posters, or the curtains and matching duvet set. For the moment her bedroom was an empty cell, waiting to be inhabited by someone else with their own sorrows and troubles.

She was dispensable, easily replaced. There were plenty of kids like her.

However, that didn't stop the police and authorities looking for her – they had a duty to do so – and while Mia had torn the SIM from her phone, she still had not managed to dispose of it. She would need to wait till she got to Inverness to detach herself from the one piece of technology that could give away her location.

HANI'S JOURNEY

Hani gazed up at the dark rolling hills enclosing them on either side. Scotland was opening up before them. The further north they travelled, the safer he felt.

"What was it like?" Mia asked him now. "The journey?"

He stared out the window but his eyes seemed to be looking at something else, an inner vision Mia could not access.

He shrugged. "We nearly drowned," he said quietly.

She was shocked into silence.

"We saw others drown..."

Mia thought of the news shots she had seen briefly on Angie and Clifford's television screen. She tended not to spend too much time down in their living room, preferring to keep to her room upstairs, but the few times she had caught the news, she remembered seeing those alien images, hard to believe, of ordinary people, dressed like herself in jeans and puffer jackets, beached up on the shore and leaping off flimsy vessels, weeping and crying. Had those rubber crafts really crossed the vast Mediterranean, braving storms and high seas? How easily would a boat like that capsize, top-heavy with passengers? It could be flipped by a freak wave, or take on board too much water until it slowly sank in the wide sea.

Hani knew.

He remembered the boat sitting improbably low in the water, weighed down with its precious human cargo. He remembered the fear inside the craft, the terror, the moaning; the crying of small children. Even a life-jacket wouldn't save them if the boat tipped or sank. The waves were so high they could not see the horizon; all they could see was water, endless grey, white-tipped foam, churning, terrifying. Acres and acres of a moving landscape that was never still, and had no visible landmarks, just a rolling desert of fathomless black that was the surface of the sea.

The bottom of the boat had filled with water. They were soaked to the skin, and everyone on board was desperate with fear, even strong men, weeping, nervously hanging on to the edge of the boat, clinging to life. It was either this, or face the bombs and the decimated streets back in Syria.

They were the lucky ones who had escaped.

Except they did not feel lucky.

And Hani knew that for him to have survived this far at all was a miracle. It didn't make him feel grateful though. He just wondered why any of it had had to happen in the first place, and more than anything he wanted his sister back. He wanted Reena's smile, her kindness, her reassurance.

None of this he could share with Mia, but somehow he did not need to. It was as if she understood already, without the need for words.

*

They managed to avoid the ticket collector throughout the entire journey to Inverness.

"I think we are getting quite good at this," Hani observed.

"Cutbacks," Mia told him, and grinned.

"What?"

She shook her head. "It doesn't matter."

But they had yet to negotiate the barrier at Inverness.

They had to change seats once or twice, and the second time they moved a middle-aged woman sat across from them. Mia thought nothing of this, at first. They kept their voices down, murmuring together, but when Mia glanced up she got the distinct impression the woman was eavesdropping on their conversation.

She was pretending to read a book, but after Hani spoke briefly about his journey, she glanced up and caught Mia's eye. She looked like a teacher, Mia decided.

After that, her eyes kept sliding towards them and there was a suspicious, officious air about her that made Mia feel distinctly uncomfortable. She had a sixth sense for that kind of thing.

She nudged Hani quietly and gestured for him to move, but as they slid out from behind their table, she could feel the teacher's eyes on them: assessing, probing. Mia didn't like it.

After that she began to feel paranoid and every time she caught a stranger's eye she felt as if she and Hani were being closely observed, wondering what they were up to, where they were going, how they knew each other. Hani looked noticeably different; his clothes were shabby and not the cleanest.

Suddenly a thought screamed at Mia inside her head and she didn't know why she hadn't realised before now.

We *look* like runaways. We look so obvious; we stick out like a sore thumb. How could anyone not grow suspicious on seeing us?

She wondered if information had already been released, descriptions issued, maybe even a sad-looking school snapshot of Mia herself?

It was possible.

The train journey to Inverness had taken three and a half hours. Perhaps that was long enough for the engines of police investigation to creak into progress. But the public were bombarded with so many news stories now, an avalanche of information that it was hardly likely that a young orphan missing from a school in Grangefield would be on anyone's mind. This thought consoled her somewhat.

They got off the train at Inverness, along with everyone else, and stared at the fortress-like barrier at the end of the platform.

"How are we going to get through *that* without a ticket?"

They waited, biding their time for a bit then Mia spotted a surge of high school students on a school trip. They filled the station with their noise and chatter. As they approached the barrier they were waved through the unlocked gate at the side by a guard while teachers stood by, laughing and joking. The guard was laughing with them, making jokes about how they had their hands full today, so Mia and Hani seized their moment. They joined the middle of the group and surged through the crush with everyone else.

They were out on the station concourse.

Free.

Mia turned to Hani, elated, and they burst out laughing.

"We did it," he said.

"Partners in crime," Mia smiled.

"I have committed no crime."

"Of course you haven't," she said quickly.

"There's no crime in wanting to survive," he said.

"Of course. That's not what I meant. It's just a phrase... what people say!"

"People say lots of things. You still need to get rid of that phone," he reminded her.

She dropped it in the nearest wastepaper bin with a wistful goodbye. "There goes our link with modern technology!"

She turned back to Hani, smiling, but the expression on his face stopped her dead in her tracks.

"What is it?" she asked.

"Don't turn round," he said.

Two policemen were scanning the station concourse. Mia heard a sound behind her, a burst of static from one of their radios.

"Maybe you didn't get rid of your phone quick enough," he said.

THE TRAIN TO NOWHERE

How they managed to evade the police officers on the station concourse, Hani still wasn't sure, but they somehow succeeded in giving them the slip and found themselves on the Far North Line, bound for Thurso and Wick, one of the northern-most points of mainland Britain.

It was an obscure stretch of branch line, barely used, and the train they were on was like something from a children's picture book, labouring its way across the moor.

Mia had purchased their tickets for £15.50 each, which meant she had only nine pounds left of the money she had stolen from Angie's purse.

As soon as they pulled out of Inverness they both sighed with relief. There were only two carriages and it was a rattling, old-fashioned affair. They crossed a broad river and headed out into more open country. River after river flowed directly beneath the juddering wheels.

"At least we've got valid tickets this time," Mia said. "No threat of being thrown off the train."

Hani nodded and stared out curiously at the dark heathery hills rolling past their window.

There was no one else on board except a woman with a shopping trolley and a man in green wellies carrying some fishing equipment.

They passed a couple of distilleries and after a place called Invershin they hit the wilds of Sutherland where the landscape grew more remote, hinting at Scotland's distant past. Nothing had changed up here; civilization had been kept at bay. They passed the gates of a huge castle then through a tiny fishing port, while the little train hugged the rugged coastline. In the distance, they could see the sinister outline of a former naval base, facing out across the ocean like a dark shadow. The surf broke so close to the edge of the rails that it was exhilarating to lean out and listen to it.

Although Hani bore a terror of the sea, this was different. It was exciting to sail along beside this dramatic coastline, virtually the only passengers on board this rickety little train, as far as they could see.

"You're a bit off the beaten track, are ye not?" the guard said, as he examined their tickets carefully.

Too carefully for Mia's liking.

"We're going to visit our grandparents," she offered neatly, "Well, *my* grandparents."

The guard glanced at them in silence; but offered no comment.

Mia inwardly cursed herself.

She could imagine him talking to the police later.

"Aye, now ye come to mention it there was something odd about the pair. I thought nothing of it at the time…"

Her mind ran cold at the thought.

He moved on, but she was left with an uneasy feeling.

After Helmsdale, the line began to snake away from

the coast towards a station called Kinbrace. Then the landscape became even wilder. Blocks of dense green Christmas trees, clumps of Scots pine, streams and burns carving a path through the boggy landscape; then a scar of white foam on a far hillside, a distant waterfall threading its way through the clefts of a gully.

Mia couldn't help feeling pleased with herself. At this rate they would find themselves at the top of Scotland before they knew it. Then they would need to trek the remainder of their journey to the ominous-sounding *Balfour House*.

What they would find when they arrived there, she did not know, but there was no way she was going to abandon Hani. If he needed to find his sister, then she would help him do it. There was no question of that.

The island would have to wait.

The open heath looked hostile and bare beneath a slowly scudding sky. Mia was exhausted after her night-time flit from Grangefield. It seemed as if so much had happened already. She felt miles away from her old life and now she was in the midst of a new adventure, one that mattered, with a friend she cared about at her side. So it was with a sense of peace that she slipped into a gentle sleep.

Hani watched her sleeping in the corner of the carriage, her head leaning against the window, but he could not join her. He was on guard, ever-vigilant. He did not trust life and he did not trust those men to leave him alone. Yusuf wanted him dead or alive. He remembered him kneeling tenderly beside him in the great carrot-topping shed and murmuring softly, "What am I going to do with you?" before placing a finger to his own temple in imitation of a gun, and pretending to quietly fire it.

Nothing haunted Hani as much as this gesture – offered so softly with a pretence at kindness. That made it worse, somehow.

The train seemed to be slowing as they neared an obscure little station that was barely a station at all. A short platform slid into view, with one word painted on a makeshift piece of board. Forsinard. As they drew closer Hani's sharp eye noticed a black jeep parked on a patch of ground not far from the platform, its engine running.

He froze. It couldn't be. He sat up straight, wiped the glass and peered closer, his mind racing. It was Yusuf. Sitting in the driver's seat, another man beside him. Instantly Hani pulled away from the window and slid down low in his seat.

He shook Mia awake and it didn't take her long to recognize the familiar look of terror in his eyes, so she followed his lead and they crawled down into the aisle, out of sight.

"I don't understand," Hani whispered, on all fours now. "How did they manage to trace us?"

"Are you sure it was them? Perhaps you're just getting paranoid…"

"I'm certain."

"Maybe they didn't see us?" Mia said hopefully, pulling a bit of stuck chewing gum from the palm of her hand. "Yuk!" But she was secretly hoping he'd been mistaken.

The train did not spend long idling in the station; when it moved off again they looked back at the parked vehicle.

It was empty.

Hani fought down feelings of nausea.

The train was so small – if Yusuf and his friend had boarded, it wouldn't take them long to find Mia and Hani. But how had they known they would be on this train?

As Hani knew, these were dangerous men, clearly intent on chasing their prey into the wilderness spaces of Scotland and catching hold of him no matter what. They did not intend to lose him, or let him go so easily.

THE LEAP

The two men entered the carriage, caught sight of Hani, and began to slowly saunter towards him.

Hani gulped.

Yusuf stared at him and opened his lips in a wolfish grin. Hani could not help staring back at his arch-enemy, the man who seemed intent on pursuing him to the end. But behind Yusuf and his friend was the guard.

"Tickets please?"

While Yusuf lifted his wallet from his pocket, Mia and Hani took the opportunity to leave the carriage.

Yusuf stared after them, distracted, and sent Karl after them.

They made their way into the next carriage, which was occupied by the only other two passengers on the train – the old woman with a shopping trolley and the man in gum boots, dressed in green waterproofs and tweed, ready for a day's fishing.

Mia led the way and they slid into a seat opposite the fisherman.

Karl sat a few yards away and glowered at them across the carriage. But neither he nor Yusuf made a move; they would bide their time, and pounce at the next opportunity.

When the guard began walking down the aisle towards them, swaying to the rattling motion of the train, Hani willed him to stay close.

Don't go, he prayed. *Please don't leave us alone with Karl or Yusuf.*

The next stop was a tiny station called *Alt-na-breac*. Here, the man in green wellies dismounted, still weighed down by his fishing tackle. Mia and Hani watched him get off and waited until the heavy door clanged shut behind him.

At the very last moment, as the train was pulling away, Mia and Hani leapt up and made a quick dash for the corridor. They had opened the door and jumped down onto the gravel of the track below before Karl had time to react. There was a shout of alarm from behind, but the train didn't stop. It kept on moving, carrying Yusuf and Karl with it. Glancing to his left, Hani felt sure he saw movement in the window, a familiar face staring out at him.

On the empty little platform, the man in gum boots was watching them.

"That was quite a stunt," he remarked.

He laughed to himself then began shouldering his fishing gear, ready to head off into the wilds.

Hani stared back at the train disappearing into the distance, waiting for a dark figure to tumble from it, but Yusuf and his friend did not make the leap. They remained on board the train, which would take them to the next station, and hopefully far enough away to give he and Mia enough of a head start.

It was the most bizarre place in the world to have a railway station. There was nothing there, apart from an abandoned ruin off to the left; and there was no road other than a worn forest track.

The fisherman turned to them with a smile. "Do you know this is the first time anyone has got off here at the same time as me?" he said.

They stared at him and Mia nodded awkwardly to show polite interest. He seemed a bit eccentric.

"It's only thanks to the Duke of Sutherland this wee station is open at all. I suppose being a Duke and all – he gets his way."

"I suppose so," Mia said tentatively.

But he hadn't finished yet. "Do you know how many passengers got off here last year?" he added.

Mia and Hani shook their heads.

"93!" He shouted. "Imagine that! 93 in one year! I ask you!"

Then he strode off down the track, smiling to himself, and disappeared between the trees.

"We should have asked him for help," Hani said.

"Nah..." Mia shook her head. "He wouldn't do anything. He'd hand us over, more like. I'm telling you. Probably nuts anyway!"

They stood for a few moments, taking in the sudden stillness. Nearby they could hear the murmur of water, tracing a route beneath marshy peatland and then the sound of a distant curlew calling.

Hani wondered how long it would take for Yusuf and his friend to dismount at the next station and retrace their movements back to this remote spot. As he stared around the open countryside, he felt the chill of being hunted. It fell over him like a shadow. Where would they hide? How fast could they run?

He saw a bird with a large wing-span – probably an eagle – coasting quietly above, observing them as it searched for its prey. It put him in mind of Yusuf and men like him.

He shuddered.

They had to move fast.

They followed the path the fisherman had taken, through the forest, listening out for any sound behind them, haunted by every cracking branch, every movement of creatures in the undergrowth.

"They'll get off the train at the next station and come back for us," Hani said,

"We'll be gone by then."

"You don't know them. They won't give up."

THE BOTHY

They left the path and cut across country into a wide open expanse of moorland, wondering how long it would take for those men to track them down. They did not know this area was called the Flow Country and that it was one of the last wildernesses in Britain.

They plunged on over the heather, while the dark came down. It was dangerous, boggy ground, and they knew they must find somewhere safe to rest before nightfall. It wouldn't be a good idea to cross such treacherous terrain in the dark.

They stopped when they reached a plateau with a commanding view of the bare slopes beneath and looked out for any sign of a jeep, or men on foot. There were no proper roads within sight – Hani and Mia had made sure of that – only dirt tracks and paths made by sheep.

The approaching darkness made them feel afraid and they wondered how they would manage to survive the night out here, all alone, without warmth or shelter, so it was with relief that they spotted a small grey bothy on the edge of a distant loch. It was barely visible against the grey of water and hillside.

They reached it just as darkness fell. The door was unlocked and opened with an eerie whine.

The bothy consisted of just one room, with a couple of hard wooden bunks, no blankets or pillows on them; but there was a small fireplace and unbelievably, a stash of dry kindling left in a bucket.

"Come on," Mia said, "We'll light a fire."

But Hani was cautious. "Wait. What if someone comes?"

"Stop worrying. I think we've lost them. For now."

He watched her in silence.

"These places are left open on purpose, for hillwalkers. It's a tradition."

"And what if there are hillwalkers out there now and they find us?"

Mia shrugged as she started to build a small fire.

"I remember my dad doing this," she murmured, "in the cottage on the island."

"You talk a lot about this island!"

They sat close to the flames and listened to the night outside.

The glow from their fire could be seen for miles, flickering between the cracks in the old wooden door. The question was whether anyone else was out there on those dark hills that night to notice.

Hani woke in the middle of the night, his thoughts turning to his sister, Reena.

He peered through a crack in the door, out into the night. The moor was spattered with the moonlit gleam of treacherous bog pools. On one side of the bothy the loch lay like glass, reflecting the sky; on the other stretched the moor.

He peered closer. He thought he could detect a single pinprick of light swaying gently from side to side in the distance. He screwed up his eyes.

There it was...

Then it vanished again.

He turned to Mia sleeping in the other bunk and thought about waking her.

In the end, he kicked over the remains of their fire, then lay down on the bunk opposite, too exhausted to worry about who or what was out there. No matter what dangers might be stealthily creeping towards them through the night, he could not stay awake any longer.

It was Hani who woke first. He was used to keeping early hours at the carrot-topping shed, standing in the dark before his station and dragging the frozen carrots towards him.

He woke Mia and they went outside into the pre-dawn light. Taking their few things with them, the clothes they slept in and Mia's small mustard backpack, they set off across the moor.

The rough heathery landscape grew pale with morning light and they trod carefully through the bog, jumping from tussock to tussock to avoid the standing water. Before long they were soaked through, tired and hungry.

They paused and Mia glanced back at the far side of the loch where she could see a tiny figure in the distance. She stood stock still and stared.

Hani followed her gaze.

"Isn't that...?"

"The man from the train!"

It was the eccentric man in green wellies who had got off at the same deserted station. He was fishing beside the loch, sitting calmly in the great expanse; a lone figure, quite content in his solitude.

"Maybe we should ask him for help?" Hani said.

But he didn't really look like the type of person you could disturb easily; he seemed so absorbed in his own solitude.

They made their way slowly towards him, and he watched them moving across the open moor.

THE ECCENTRIC FISHERMAN

He had shrewd eyes that watched them carefully, making no judgements.

"Good morning. You again?" was all he said.

Hani stood there tongue-tied, suddenly not knowing what to say. Mia was no help. She didn't seem able to speak either.

"Hungry?" he asked them. "Well, you're in luck, as it happens."

He leaned over and produced a thermos flask filled with hot tea and a packet of biscuits.

"There's more where that came from." He gestured at a neat metal box which contained his gas stove and a folding kettle. "Always come prepared."

"What are you fishing for?" Hani asked.

"Salmon, mostly." He behaved as if it was the most natural thing in the world to encounter two scruffy and frightened-looking teenagers in the middle of nowhere, on the run by the looks of things, from men they were afraid of.

Hani and Mia drank their hot tea and devoured the biscuits, and as they did so they felt safer, being close to the eccentric fisherman. So many adults wanted to take things from them, tell them what to do, control their lives, knowing what was best for them, but he seemed different somehow. He simply let them be, waiting for them to tell him what they were doing out here.

"Where are you heading?" he asked eventually.

Hani didn't reply, but Mia said "Coll. It's an island," she added self-consciously.

"Ah… that's more to the west," he pointed out.

"I know. We're doing a detour."

"Trying to get away from those men on the train, no doubt. Nasty-looking pair."

Hani glanced at the man quickly: something made him hesitate. Why did he want to know where they were going? Could they trust him?

"Hey up!" he said calmly, as his line tugged in the water. He began to reel in his catch. A fat pink salmon was his reward for patience, dangling in mid-air, its gleaming skin shining. They watched its thrashing death throes as he landed it safely on the bank, and detached it from the hook with careful fingers. He roasted it in foil over a small fire and shared it with them. Mia thought she had never tasted anything so good, the thick oily flesh flaking away between her fingers. Hani ate steadily and quietly, stopping when he had had enough. There was an air of sadness about him always, sitting over him like a cloud – all that he had lived through, all that he had been through, and all that he had lost and left behind… none of which he could share.

The fisherman watched the two young people carefully.

"Well, I guess you have your reasons for being out here," he offered quietly, waiting for them to speak.

Hani and Mia kept quiet, neither willing to share their story.

The morning light grew stronger and the contours of the land became sharper until they could see for miles. This made them nervous, for it also meant they could be seen for miles, too.

"I think we need to get on our way," Mia said, wiping her hands in the grass to clean them.

The fisherman looked disappointed, as if he had not quite fulfilled his potential in some way.

"There's a large house you could head towards, big grey stone structure on the edge of a plantation of trees. You could head there if you like... due north west, if you can find it. You'd find shelter there."

Hani stared at him. "What do you mean?"

The fisherman frowned and touched his hat. "Just what I say!"

It was an odd reply.

"Thank you for the tea and the salmon. It was delicious," Mia said.

Hani nodded and offered the fisherman his hand. He shook it.

"Good luck," he said, and watched them head off into the uplands.

They left him beside his peaceful loch, where he sat staring out at the shining surface of the water. Before long he began to blend into the grey of the rocks behind him.

*

It was hard going, trying to avoid the bogs, but it grew easier once they reached higher ground.

They stopped briefly for a rest and sat on a stone, gazing down at the landscape below. Hani focussed on the sky and the clouds, but Mia's gaze was fixed on something else.

She nudged him.

"Is it my imagination, or...?"

Hani followed her gaze. She was right. Two figures moving below.

They dropped on their bellies and peered down between tufts of heather. Men advancing steadily across the moor.

"Perhaps they're just hillwalkers." Mia said, but neither of them believed that. There was something about the set purpose of their gait, the way they were so dogged and determined.

They looked around desperately. There was nowhere to hide. They were surrounded by nothing but bare slopes, where any movement would be detected a mile away. Hani remembered learning about how a mountain hare will lie down in its set, a hollow shaped exactly like the creature itself, so that it could not be seen except from the air. Should they try to do the same? Just lie still and merge into the hillside?

Craning his neck, he could tell they were on a false summit, but there were other higher summits above them. Crouching, they made their way around the side of the hill. Behind this was a gully of sorts and it occurred to them they could put this gully between themselves and their enemies and even double back on their tracks; try to fool them that way.

So that is what they did.

They pushed on around the side of the hill, plunged down into the gully, splashed their way across a burn and scrambled up the other side, grabbing at rocks and branches.

They glanced back. They had succeeded in putting a deep glen between themselves and their enemies, but they pushed on, still out in the open. Up ahead they could see a ruined wall, blocks of masonry left in a pile, and reached it just as they saw two dark figures topping the far ridge. They dropped down behind the ruin, breath rasping in panic. They could almost feel the eyes of their enemy sweeping the landscape, trying to discern any tiny movement which would indicate the presence of their prey.

They kept very still and waited.

In the sky above them Hani saw the eagle again, stretching its wide wings and releasing a hungry cry.

He and Mia were the hunted; they were the prey.

Those men wanted Hani back and they wanted him badly. They would not let him disappear, vanish into a normal life. He had been purchased; he was bought goods and if they did not keep a hold of him, there were even more dangerous men who would make Yusuf and his friends pay the price.

There was a price on Hani's head...

THE CAVE

He could feel the heather scratching his face and there was a peaty smell in his nostrils; a scent like honey. They had managed to put a gully between themselves and Yusuf but still they were not safe.

The men would have to plunge down into the burn in order to reach their prey and then climb their way back up.

Hani peered stealthily through a gap between the stones, keeping his head low.

There they were. He ducked down. He could see them clearly now. They were scanning the landscape around them. It looked like they were discussing their options before beginning to head on up the steep slope.

"How did they know we were here?"

"They must have been tracking us all along."

Mia looked at Hani and murmured, "They must want you very badly."

Hani waited, his lips close to the heather and grasses growing between the fallen stones, tufts of bog cotton trembling in the breeze.

He was too afraid to speak.

"Come on," Mia said, breaking free from the ruin once the men were out of sight. "We don't have much time."

It wouldn't take long for the men to realise they'd been fooled and retrace their steps.

Mia and Hani double-backed on their own tracks, scrambling down into the steep gully until they were out of sight. Rocks and stones slithered and fell away beneath their feet.

At the bottom of the chasm was a stream.

They followed this carefully between the steep hillsides. The murmur of the water drowned any other sound. Hani glanced nervously above him, fearing to see a dark figure appear on the ridge above.

They would be sitting ducks if they were spotted, trapped inside this natural fissure in the landscape, tall rock faces either side hemming them in.

They heard the thunder of a waterfall up ahead before they saw it. Its roar grew louder, then Hani spotted a dark opening in the cliff face above them. Grabbing Mia's shoulder, he pointed upwards.

A black hole in the hillside, a small indented shelf, overhung by vines and creeper, the undergrowth almost obscuring it from view. Except it was not a shelf. It was a cave.

They craned their necks.

Could they manage it?

They looked back down the gully, the way they had come, where the men might appear at any second.

They nodded and began to climb, very slowly and steadily at first, using the black rocks and the ivy as footholds. Hand over hand they climbed. Cool green ferns brushed their faces, the roar of the waterfall in their ears.

Mia almost lost her grip when a small boulder

scudded away from beneath her foot, but Hani grabbed her from above and she held on tight to the rock face like a limpet.

Gradually, by slow degrees, they reached the dark hole they had spied from below; a cave, obscured by greenery.

They crawled inside its cool darkness and hid.

Like hunted animals.

They crept away from the entrance and waited.

Yusuf and his friend kept searching. They were fit and strong and they were desperate to catch their prey. They had found the fisherman earlier and questioned him, but the man informed them he had been there all night and all morning and no one had come that way; he was sure of it.

This raised doubts in Yusuf's mind.

They had seen the two figures for themselves, climbing upwards. Maybe the old man had not been observant enough and failed to notice them, keeping his eyes fixed instead on his line and what lay beneath the surface of the loch. Either that or he was lying.

They hurried on up the hillside until they came to the summit, where they could see all the summits beyond that, as the land rose and fell.

They hesitated.

Should they press on?

Yusuf's friend, Karl, nudged him and indicated the gully below, where a stream ran along the bottom, carving a deep channel through the hills.

Yusuf nodded and they began to make their way down.

Soon they found themselves splashing through a narrow burn, steep rock faces either side of them.

The roar of the water grew louder as they approached the waterfall.

Yusuf glanced up briefly at the hollows in the rock face. Stood still and listened.

His eagle gaze swept the rock face, focussing for a moment on a black hole halfway up, obscured by a curtain of green vines. He narrowed his eyes and sniffed the air, for all the world like a wolf in search of its prey.

Inside the cave, Hani and Mia waited. They looked at each other in the semi-darkness, and blinked.

Their silence spoke volumes.

They were terrified that Yusuf and Karl would look up and glimpse the shallow darkness of the cave. And if they did notice it, would it occur to them that Hani and Mia might climb this high and choose to hide just here, in a narrow cleft next to a waterfall?

Above the roar of water, they heard one of the men curse when he was directly below, as he stumbled and fell against the slippery rocks.

Long moments passed.

Then the men ploughed on, intent on their mission to find their quarry.

They had hunted the boy down and they knew they had him trapped. He must be around here somewhere.

They walked directly beneath the cave, their eyes focussing on the difficulties of negotiating the ground beneath their feet, the smooth boulders and rocks, slick with moss.

The curtain of ivy draped across the cave entrance kept Hani and Mia safe for now. They could only be glimpsed from a certain angle and once that angle was passed, they became invisible again.

At one point the men encountered the carcase of a dead sheep, rotting between the stones and the stench was overpowering. They covered their mouths, gagged, and moved on.

Inside their cave, Mia and Hani did not dare to believe that they might have outwitted them.

An hour passed, sitting crouched in the darkness, side by side like two owls, peering out from their eyrie at the greenery below.

They thought it best to wait, in case Yusuf and Karl decided to retrace their steps.

Perhaps they wouldn't? Perhaps they would just plough on, into the hills? But Hani and Mia had no way of knowing. At least they could rest here, undisturbed for now. Neither of them relished the thought of climbing out and having to renegotiate the steep sides of that rock face again.

"We could stay here forever," Mia breathed. "Hide away from the world."

Hani looked at her in silence.

The world was a cruel place. He wondered for a

moment what Mia was running from, what life was like for her back in Grangefield with Angie and Clifford. This dark cave held a certain comfort for them both, despite the cold seeping from the stones.

"I think it should be safe now," Mia whispered. "They've gone."

They were about to emerge when they heard voices below. The men were returning, retracing their steps. Hani pushed Mia backwards into the darkness of the cave.

"That was a close shave," she whispered.

Hani was quiet for a bit, then frowned. "Shave?"

"It's a figure of speech," Mia said. "Don't worry about it."

He nodded sagely. "You teach me lots of new words, Mia."

"Maybe now isn't the time for an English lesson."

Hani peered through the curtain of ivy, watching his enemies stumbling away down the riverbed.

They waited until the men were out of sight, another half hour or so of sitting quietly inside their elevated cave.

HUNTED

Hours later, bone-tired and weary, they trudged along an upper glen, a high plateau.

They were making an attempt to head to the north-west, on the advice of their friend, the eccentric fisherman.

Quiet streams rumbled beneath the peat. It was a desolate landscape where no one lived, and where birds of prey ruled the sky.

At another time they might have enjoyed the landscape, the extreme solitude and tranquillity, but right now they did not feel very tranquil. The only sound apart from the murmur of a nearby burn and the gentle breeze through the grasses, was the voice of a skylark in the wide sky above.

It was beautiful.

But then they heard something else which made them pause and hesitate.

A faint beat on the air.

They tensed.

They saw it circling far below, hanging over its own black shadow, wheeling like a hawk. A helicopter scanning the hills below.

Hani and Mia leapt up. Could those men, or Uncle

Giorgio, have access to such a thing? Or was it the police, after Mia?

It was still far below them, making slow progress, trying to cover each patch of ground methodically.

Now they were being hunted from the air.

They had to get out of the open before it was too late and the chopper was upon them, but there was nowhere to hide.

In the distance, they could see a clump of unnatural-looking trees planted halfway down a hillside to their left and as they made their way towards it, they caught sight of a cluster of tall grey chimneys on the far side of the treetops.

They had no choice.

They had to get out of the open.

So they crashed their way into the densely-packed plantation, where the firs grew close together, and the ground was carpeted with soft brown needles. Here there was decay, and silence.

But invading that silence was the distant beat of the chopper, still far away, but growing steadily closer.

This was the only cover to be had for miles around.

ANOTHER CHANCE ENCOUNTER

Mia and Hani ran through the undergrowth, pushing aside branches that swept their bare faces like feathery hands. When they reached the edge, they stared out across an open expanse, too rough to be called a lawn. Before them was the façade of a great house with several chimneys, tall windows reflecting the light.

Perhaps this was the house the fisherman had mentioned. Due north-west he had said, and there was certainly no other building or structure for miles around.

Far away they could hear the thunder of the helicopter growing steadily closer. Their hearts beating inside their chests, they ran across the lawn, up the steps, and were about to bang on the door for admittance, but there was no need.

The great oak door swung open on its hinges, almost as if they were expected.

A huge stone-flagged hallway stretched before them, a baronial manor of some kind, but it did not look very lived in.

Their footsteps echoed in the hollow space and Mia's voice rang out against the stone walls as she called out.

"Hello?"

No one answered, except her own echo. Then there

was the flutter of a wood pigeon as it burst from a side room and soared above their heads and out of the door.

She ducked and screamed, then brushed herself down afterwards, feeling slightly silly.

"Must have come in through a broken window," Hani said.

They proceeded carefully and quietly through the house, stepping gingerly.

"Hello?" she called again, as they entered each room, but still no one answered. Hani followed, letting her lead the way.

It was as if the place wasn't properly lived in. What furniture there was looked old and dusty, neglected somehow. Old picture frames hung askew on their hooks; a suit of polished armour stood only half to attention, as if it had once been knocked sideways and never corrected.

The fireplaces were full of old ash.

Mia put her foot on the bottom step and creaked her way up the broad oak staircase, her hand sliding along the banister, wondering what she would find above. Hani followed.

A long corridor led to an open door at the far end where light spilled out. Something drew her on. When she reached the open door she could see where the light was coming from. Wide windows commanded a view of the moor beneath. The room was lined with books and there was a massive stone fireplace; this one was lit.

Beside the fireplace was a man, seated in a winged leather armchair lifting a glass to his lips. And they knew the man.

It was their eccentric fisherman from the loch below.

They stared at him.

He stared back.

"I was wondering when you'd turn up. I'm glad you found it."

He saw them glance nervously towards the window where the regular beat of the chopper was creeping steadily closer.

"Friends of yours, are they?" he asked.

"Not exactly," Mia said.

Hani shook his head, his eyes dark with unhappiness.

"They are my enemies. They took my sister and they want to take me too."

The man's eyes narrowed and he bit his lip.

"Well, we can't have that now, can we?" he leaned forward, putting his weight on the armrests of his stout leather armchair, and pulled himself upright.

"I've had a good morning's fishing, as it happens, but I thought it was time to call it a day. Now... I'm no expert, but I have a suspicion those gentlemen might alight near here and choose to pay us a visit... or pay *me* a visit, rather. I've met them before as a matter of fact... or friends of theirs, anyway."

He looked at them both hard. "I don't need to know what you've done... or what you haven't done."

All three of them stood in front of the huge windows, staring out at the moor and the hills beyond. Suddenly, from beyond the trees, burst the ugly snout of the helicopter. It circled above the house, juddering the air, deafening them; the branches of the trees swayed and bent backwards as the blades of the chopper cut the air. Hani and Mia cowered away from the window, but the chopper passed on, continuing to search the surrounding

110

area. They could hear it overhead, advancing and retreating and advancing again, swirling round and round.

When it finally decided to land in the space in front of the house, Hani felt himself gripped by terror. How would their new friend manage to hide them now, or keep these dangerous men at bay?

It seemed they had run out of luck. And what would happen to them once they were taken captive? Hani would be returned to the carrot-topping factory – or worse. And Mia would be handed back to Angie and Clifford whether she liked it or not.

The fisherman's face grew stern. "Come this way," he beckoned them along the hallway and they clattered down the stairs to the floor below.

He opened an obscure little door in the wooden panelling under the stairs. "Before you go, take these," and he thrust a thick warm coat at them and a bundle of dry clothes. Then he took them down a further flight, a secret staircase which led underground.

"Help me," he muttered, "quickly," as he began to drag a stout wooden cupboard away from the wall. They helped him to push the heavy piece across the flags and behind it a narrow archway was revealed in the brickwork.

The old man wheezed for a moment as he caught his breath.

"You can follow this tunnel as far as it takes you."

He reached behind to a shelf, lifted up an old-fashioned glass oil lantern and lit it for them with his lighter.

"Take this."

They stared at him, their eyes wide in the light from the lantern.

"Now – go!"

"Thank you," Hani mumbled and Mia reached up and kissed the old man on the cheek.

He shook his head dismissively, as if such a display of affection was not called for. Then he watched them duck their heads and disappear into the darkness of the tunnel.

Once they had gone, he tried to push the heavy oak cupboard back into place across the entrance, but it would not budge. He was not strong enough. He would have to take his chances that his new visitors would not search below or find the secret staircase. Then he wiped his hands and steadily climbed the stairs.

He was walking the length of the flagged hallway in time to hear his visitors bang on the open door.

THE TUNNEL

Mia held the lantern high; its light fell fitfully on the black walls either side and into the darkness ahead. Hani followed her close behind.

The walls were dry at first, but after a while they could hear the plash of water underfoot. They kept trudging steadily forward.

They wondered what was happening to their new friend up above and how he was managing to put Yusuf and his gang off the scent. He had been so kind…

"Who are those people in the chopper?" Mia asked.

Hani shrugged. "Yusuf and Karl. Or maybe Uncle Giorgio."

"Who?"

"He was the man who found us in the Calais jungle. Remember I told you?"

Mia was silent, listening to his sad little voice in the shadows.

"He told us that if we worked for him, we would be safe. We would have a home, a future. That is what our parents believed."

Mia did not know what to say. "Maybe it's not them at all in the helicopter. It might be the police… I'm a thief, remember. I stole Angie's money…"

Minutes passed, and they struggled on through the darkness.

"Why did you run away from them?" Hani asked.

Mia shrugged.

"Did they treat you badly? Did they beat you?"

"No," she said. "But – they didn't care. Funny isn't it? Carers are supposed to care. I was just another number to fill a bed. They got money for looking after me. They spent it on doing an extension. They pretended all the time."

Hani listened, trying to understand.

"They pretended to be something they weren't. They spoke to teachers and social workers as if they knew what was best for me, but always they seemed to be saying that it was my fault I ended up alone. All of them! Social workers, teachers, foster carers. They filled in reports, had meetings with each other, talked about me all the time as if I was a problem rather than a person. Kids like me, we keep people like them in a job."

There was a short silence. Mia realised she had never been able to speak so candidly before and it was a slight weight off her shoulders to talk about it.

"Was it always like that?" Hani asked now.

She shook her head. "No!"

She saw a white curving beach in her mind, waves hissing on the sand. A woman laughing, her long hair blowing back in the wind, a man in the background – her dad – holding a camera. She often wondered where those pictures had gone. No one had made sure she kept anything.

There *had* been a time before the world had become a dark and lonely place, but it was hard to reach. All she

114

knew was that she had to get to the island one day. If she could get there, then she would be safe. She could reconnect with her own past and then – and only then – would it feel as if she had a future.

"I wonder how long this tunnel is?" Hani said, suddenly nervous at the thought that their lantern might run out of oil before they ran out of tunnel.

It was unnerving, having to keep walking into the unknown. The old man had given them no indication as to where it would lead – only that they should keep going until the end. It occurred to them both they had been very quick to trust him, but then, what choice did they have?

"Who was he?" Hani said out loud, after a while, echoing Mia's own thoughts.

She remembered his cheerful and eccentric demeanour as he headed off down the forest track at the remote railway station at *Alt-na-breac* where they had first encountered him; how he had stopped, registered their presence behind him and said, "It's only thanks to the Duke of Sutherland that this railway line exists at all. Bit of a railway enthusiast. I suppose when you're a duke and all, you tend to get your own way."

The words came back to her now.

He lived in a massive grey stone house that stood all alone in the wilds and seemed only half-lived in, as if he spent very little time there. Perhaps it was his hideout, his private getaway, where no one could find him...

"He's a duke," Mia burst out.

"What?" Hani stumbled into the back of her. "What did you say?"

"The old man. He's the Duke of Sutherland. I'm sure of it."

"The Duke of...?" Hani didn't understand.

Mia laughed. "He's a posh geezer – someone who owns all the land. But maybe, just maybe, he's not so bad after all."

The tunnel stretched before them, with no end in sight.

They pressed on doggedly through the darkness, hoping against hope that the old Duke – if that's who he was – had managed to hide the secret tunnel, and that the men in the chopper – whoever they were – had not hurt him in any way.

ANOTHER NIGHT IN THE OPEN

The lantern was still burning when they emerged from the tunnel, which was just as well because night had fallen. As they crawled through the narrow space they began to see a pale gleam a hundred yards ahead, a kind of lightening of the air and knew the end was in sight.

They crawled out onto the dark moor and lifted the lantern high.

There was a full moon, but a wind was blowing and dark clouds scudded across it.

They walked for a long time through the darkness until they felt themselves weak with exhaustion. Up ahead they could see a low structure of some kind, so they made towards it. It was clearly a ruin, the roof and windows missing, staring like empty eye sockets. Rubble was scattered around the base of a chimney breast.

They crawled in between the broken walls and rested in a corner, against the stones, out of the wind. Mia placed the lantern on a rock and watched its light play over the ruins. Hani looked up. Above them stars wheeled in the darkness. The vast universe and their tiny circle of light – that's what it felt like.

He could hear Mia beside him, rustling in the darkness. She took out two huge knitted sweaters, pulled one on and handed the other to Hani, then found the biscuits the Duke had slipped them and tore the packet open. They sat back to back for comfort, munching. Afterwards, feeling slightly sick but full of sugar and oats, Mia closed her eyes, feeling Hani's warmth at her back.

It was obvious that Yusuf and his men knew they were still out here, wandering about on foot, maybe even the police did too.

How much longer could they hope to remain free?

Mia did not want to go back to her old life in Grangefield, lessons in that grey school with the echoing corridors, getting bullied for being small and 'in care'; living with Angie and Clifford in the shadow of a town she hated, where a giant petrochemical plant blinked and flared all night long like a futuristic monster. Sometimes they would set off a siren to warn residents to shut all their windows and doors because of a chemical leak. All of that was a far cry from what life on the island was like, a long time ago...

She wanted to stay with Hani, on the run, even if that meant being a homeless outcast.

The police will want me for theft. The thought popped into her head. She would end up being treated like a criminal instead of what she really was, a child running away because she was unhappy where she was.

"When we get to the island," Mia whispered, "You'll see the difference. You'll see how much better life will become."

Hani listened in silence.

"Everything will make sense then. When we get to the island."

She was speaking almost to herself, but Hani took

118

comfort in her words. He listened to her voice as she described the soft white beaches with the machair growing behind them, the white curve of the bay; the breezes blowing through the wildflowers, the sea stretching far away into the distance and curling inwards. Not the sea like Hani had known it, terrifying and vast, the wild Mediterranean with its hurricane temperament, swallowing boatloads full of people... but something different, something safer. He felt it because Mia described it to him so well, the home of her childhood, the place she remembered visiting when she was small and had two parents to love her... before she had to learn to fend for herself.

"We're both survivors – you and me," Mia said quietly, staring up at the dark sky through the roofless ruin.

Hani said nothing. He was thinking about the corpses he'd seen floating in the water, washed up on the shore. These were images he wanted never to see again, that he would never share or talk about. He had seen their sad porcelain faces pressed flat against the sand, lifeless like mannequins or plastic models, all the life and spirit taken from them.

But Mia was right. They were survivors. And this is what it meant to survive; it meant being haunted, carrying images you would rather not carry, but there it was, you had no choice. You had to keep going, you had to keep believing, and you had to try not to remember all the bad stuff when you shut your eyes.

Mia rested her head on Hani's shoulder and they went to sleep like that, forgetting to put out the lantern, so that its light spilled all around them, through the boulders and the cracks in the broken walls, gleaming yellow in the dark.

Far away across the moor a man stood on a high ridge, staring out at the darkness.

There was one speck in that darkness that drew his eye.

It was the sight of the tiny yellow lantern, swaying back and forth then coming to rest in a single spot, where it appeared to flicker, as it played fitfully against the stones of the ruin.

Uncle Giorgio nodded.

He was a hunter.

He hunted prey.

This is what he did for a living, how he made his way in the world.

And he had his quarry in his sights.

"*The little children will come to me*," he murmured in a low sinister voice and then laughed.

Yusuf, who was standing beside him, glanced at him uneasily.

There were times when even Yusuf was surprised by the extent of his boss's twisted mind. And Yusuf was not a man of compassion.

In his book-lined library the Duke stood at the window and looked out into the darkness. He hoped his friends had found the tunnel to be of use, and managed to avoid their pursuers.

He hadn't trusted those men. One of them was particularly urbane and polite, but the old man could see straight through that performance; he knew it wasn't genuine.

He thought of the boy Hani and wondered what his story was. The young people had not had time to share it with him, but he knew they needed help, so when the police had turned up a few hours later, asking questions, he didn't know what to think.

"We're looking for two children," one of the police officers had said. "We believe they could be in trouble."

The Duke eyed them suspiciously.

"What kind of trouble?"

The police officer smiled and said, "I'm afraid we're not at liberty to divulge that, sir. Suffice it to say they need our help."

"Why? What have they done?"

Again, the police officer was evasive.

"You're not the first visitors I've had today, as a matter of fact," the old man said.

"Oh?"

The Duke lowered his eyes. He didn't trust these two police officers either. If the young people had felt the need to run away from the authorities, then perhaps they had good reason to.

He nodded. "Yes, some unpleasant-looking types landed here in a helicopter not so long ago – believe it or not – asking similar questions as yourself."

They looked at him, startled.

"I told them the same thing as I told you. I haven't seen anyone, apart from yourselves, in the last twenty-four hours. I've never known the moor to be quite this busy before. It's usually a very remote spot. Nice and quiet, as you can imagine. I'm not used to helicopters dropping in uninvited. Or the local constabulary turning up at my door."

"We're not the local constabulary," the officer said. "We're C.I.D."

"Really? And yet you won't tell me why those two young people are in trouble or what they might be running from?"

The officer eyed the Duke suspiciously. "So you *have* come across them then?"

The old man gulped uneasily. "I'm not at liberty to divulge that, sir," he replied.

The officer raised his eyebrows and smirked, then turned to his companion who continued, "You realise it is an offence to withhold information, sir? And you certainly won't be helping those two young people by hiding them."

"I'm not hiding them. And I know one thing, if they felt the need to keep running, they must have had their reasons. Detention centres, deportation. You people should be ashamed of yourselves," the Duke burst out, suddenly unable to contain himself any longer.

"Do you mind if we take a look around, sir?" the officer asked, staring past the Duke's shoulder into the darkness of the hallway beyond.

The Duke thought about it, hesitated for a moment, then opened the door wide. "Be my guest."

The officers searched the large house tentatively, room by room, their footsteps echoing along the corridors.

The Duke stood downstairs in the hallway, listening.

The men stomped downstairs, and were about to

leave, when one of them glanced behind the Duke and noticed the door under the stairs, the one that led to the cellar.

"Excuse me, sir. May I see inside there?"

"Of course."

The old man moved aside and the officers entered the cellar. He waited several minutes, until they reappeared, frowning.

One of them handed the Duke a small school snapshot which was undeniably a picture of Mia.

"A young girl, about five foot tall," the officer began, "skinny with short hair. She seems to have got herself mixed up with a refugee boy, shabbily dressed – five foot three maybe, probably illegal. If you do see or hear of two young people at all, answering to this description, get in touch."

The old man nodded. "I'll be sure to. As you can imagine, we don't get a lot of passing traffic."

Then he watched the men retire to their vehicle and reverse away from the house. Their headlights crawled along the rutted track, several miles long, that passed for a drive, and then swung out and round onto the gravel road which cut across the moor.

Now, as he stood looking out at the dark, he hoped that Hani and Mia would get as far away from all of these men as they possibly could, for none of them seemed to have the young people's best interests at heart, as far as he could see. You could tell that, just by looking at them.

He stared out across the moor. As the moon appeared from behind heavy cloud, it caught the oily black gleam of the bog water lying low between the high tussocks of heather, and he wondered for a moment if it had been wise to let the two children go on alone.

Could he have sheltered them here?

But for how long?

They seemed to have the whole world on their trail…

Hani and Mia woke at dawn, and watched a low-lying mist drag itself across the moor. It was eerie, yet beautiful, as beams of early sunlight shot through the misty veil.

They had nothing to eat, having devoured the packet of biscuits the night before. So they stirred themselves, left the ruin and began to walk towards the line of hills in the distance.

They walked all day, and saw no one.

It did occur to them once or twice to double back and find the Duke again. Mia knew they needed help in finding Hani's sister, and locating that faraway place on the coast, Balnakeil Bay. They couldn't do it alone, but it took courage to trust a man like that. He owned property and wealth. If he found out she was a thief and a liar he would send her back to Grangefield, just like all the rest, so they kept walking, away from the Duke and the safety of his house.

The Duke had spent a restless night in his old house on the moor, surrounded by his books and his empty rooms and unlit fireplaces. The long corridors held shadows of former lives lived here long ago, and the old man could not sleep.

He was thinking about those two children, and was uneasy in his mind.

He had given them food and clothing, and an escape route from the men pursuing them (two sets of men, for heaven's sake!) but could he have done more?

He blinked out at the first light of morning from an upstairs window, and decided to take matters into his own hands.

The moor was vast, stretching from east to west, north to south, either side of his ancient mansion with its belt of trees and fir plantation around it. To find them again would be like searching for a needle in a haystack.

How could they possibly survive out there?

It would take more than a packet of biscuits and a new overcoat to keep them safe.

The Duke's mind was made up.

He liked an adventure.

He pulled on his waders and gum boots, strapped his usual fishing gear to his back, and headed off onto the moor. If anyone asked, he was fishing.

THE FARMHOUSE

Hani and Mia had reached a small summit and far beneath them they spotted one white house in the distance, a farmhouse, with dogs barking outside.

They exchanged looks and instinctively began to head down the hillside towards it.

A long white gravel road snaked away from the farm across the valley below, and disappeared over the next ridge. That road would lead somewhere, back to civilisation of some kind.

Hani grabbed Mia's arm and they dropped beside a boulder, just as a familiar black jeep began to nose its way along the track. Keeping their heads low, they watched as two men climbed out the vehicle and stood at the kitchen door asking questions. The farmer stood on his threshold, shaking his head.

As the men walked back towards the jeep, one of them happened to glance up at the hillside briefly. Hani felt his skin crawl. Yusuf. He felt as if Yusuf was peering right at him. But the men turned, got back in their jeep, and drove away.

Hani leaned back against the rock and watched the ugly black jeep vanish over the next ridge.

Mia was about to get up, but he stopped her.

"Wait. Not yet."

She slid back down beside him.

They waited for another few minutes.

There were outbuildings and barns gathered around the farmhouse and they watched as a man appeared from a side door and started up a small tractor. Two black and white collies jumped into the rear as he sped off over the fields towards his sheep scattered on the hillside.

Hani and Mia watched in silence.

The farmhouse stood empty, as far as they knew.

In that farmhouse, they might find food.

They watched the quadbike and trailer disappear over the ridge then began to make their way cautiously down the hillside. This was the first sight of civilisation they had seen in a while and they had to take a risk.

The farmyard was empty and quiet when they got there, with a few chickens scratching about in the dust. There were large barns either side, made of corrugated iron, and in these they could hear the low keening of a tethered bull.

They pushed open the wide five-barred gate into the yard and paused, listening.

As they did so another figure emerged suddenly from the dark interior of the farmhouse. She stopped and stared.

"You're trespassing," the woman announced coldly.

When they didn't reply, she shook her head slightly from side to side. Her next words took them by surprise. "You hungry?"

It was the second time someone had asked them that. Hani nodded eagerly, and Mia joined him.

They were beyond niceties.

The woman stepped aside and invited them into the kitchen where warm smells of an earlier breakfast wafted.

"Sit," she commanded them and they both sat down obediently at the kitchen table. It was covered with a red checked oilcloth, which had been wiped and cleaned so many times it was slightly sticky and moulded to the shape of the table.

"I'm not going to ask," she said.

They looked at her, wide-eyed.

"I'm not going to ask where you're from, or why you're here."

She glanced at Hani then, and his face – streaked with dirt and tiredness and sadness – seemed to tell her everything she needed to know.

Those men who had come asking questions… she had not trusted or liked them, not one inch, and she did not believe anything they had said.

How Hani had ended up here, she had no idea, but she knew when a child was hungry.

They watched her in silence as she filled the kettle at the sink, set it on the hob and lit the gas.

Then they watched as she broke eggs into a frying pan.

"You like mushrooms and tomatoes?" she asked.

They nodded.

"You don't look like you can afford to be choosy, at any rate. We don't often get strange kids turning up in our yard, just wandering in off the moor," she added, placing steaming mugs of hot tea in front of them. "As you can imagine. But I watch the news. And I think I can hazard a guess where you're from," she gestured at Hani in particular, and he lowered his eyes.

She was strangely direct and up front for someone who lived so far away from other people, but perhaps that was why. Her isolated home meant she didn't have time for chit-chat; she just cut straight to the facts.

"My name is Elizabeth, by the way. Beth, for short."

She looked at them both, waiting. "I don't necessarily expect you to tell me yours. It's obvious you don't really want people to know who you are, by the looks of things."

She seemed to be so adept at putting words into their mouths that it robbed them of the need to speak and there was a certain relief in that. They had nothing to say. Silence was a welcome refuge after everything they had both been through.

She sat down at the table and watched them eat.

They were so hungry they devoured every mouthful without looking up. Hani had not enjoyed a hot meal on a decent plate since leaving his home in Aleppo what seemed like a hundred years ago.

The woman took pleasure in seeing them wipe their plates clean and gave a grudging smile. There was something hard-edged and reluctant about her kindness, as if it was not easily given. She seemed proud and self-contained. She wasn't effusive, but she was honest.

She sat with her elbows on the table.

Mia's eyes travelled around the room and came to rest on a photograph on the dresser; a young boy about Hani's age, staring solemnly out at the camera as if he knew what destiny had in store for him.

The woman followed Mia's gaze. "That was my son."

Her eyes filled with a desperate but stoical sadness. So that was why she had looked at Hani in that way; why she wanted to feed him, help him, nurture him, if only for an hour or two.

A whole story unfolded in that shabby farmhouse kitchen, with cups and plates piled in the sink, the photograph on the dresser, the egg remains congealing in the pan.

Everyone has a story, Mia thought then. Some people land on the squares with ladders leading to a bright new future, others land on the ones with the snakes, sliding back down into disaster and disappointment; that's all, she thought. There is no rhyme or reason behind it, no grand benevolent scheme. We take what we are given and we run with it. And if we are lucky, we survive. That seemed like a hard lesson to learn, but she realised that both she and Hani knew it off by heart. That's what they had in common. Misfortune. Squares with snakes on them.

Like Hani, she did not want prison walls; she wanted fresh air and freedom. She wanted an island of safety with its open beaches and the wind blowing free through the machair.

If the police caught Hani, he would end up in a detention centre. He was an illegal 'migrant' – that word they so enjoyed handing around – without passport or papers. Uncle Giorgio and the traffickers had kept his paperwork. They had taken his mother's money and left him with nothing – not even a future.

If Uncle Giorgio and Yusuf caught Hani, they would drag him back to the carrot-topping shed, or worse...

they would kill him. And they would kill his sister Reena too, if they had not already done so.

What would they do to Mia? Would they destroy her dreams?

Hani realised then that he wanted very much to help Mia reach her island. If it was important to her, then it was important to him. But first, they had to find Reena.

"I am looking for my sister, Reena," Hani said suddenly, looking up from his plate at the woman.

She looked around the room, half-puzzled.

"You'll not find her here."

"They took her. To a place up north. On the coast."

The woman leaned forward intently and listened.

"Who took her?"

But Hani went quiet; he did not want to say. He didn't even have the words for it, for how do you explain in polite conversation to people who have never known such things, the evil of men like Yusuf and Karl and Uncle Giorgio, who sell people for a living?

Human traffickers… that was the word… but it was not a word you could say with ease in a place like this farmhouse kitchen with its domestic clutter on the shelves and worktop. It sounded too bizarre, out of place.

"Go on," she said quietly. "I'm listening."

And they tried to tell her.

"We need to travel north, to Balnakeil Bay on the north coast, and find a place called *Balfour House*. We think that's where they have Reena. If…" Mia stopped herself. She had been about to add "if she's still alive."

"Could the police not help you with any of this?" Beth said.

131

Mia and Hani looked at her and the trust they felt evaporated, just like that. Perhaps they had said too much already. Perhaps she would contact her local police officer in a well-meaning attempt to help them, without realising the consequences that would follow. They would be separated; Mia would be returned to Angie and Clifford and to her life in Grangefield within sight of the Monster; Hani would be detained on the grounds of being an illegal immigrant, and Reena would be lost forever. They would never find her again.

"NO!" Hani looked at Beth and the stark panic in his eyes stopped her in her tracks. "You must tell no one. It wouldn't help."

"Hani would end up being held somewhere, or sent back to Syria, and he would never see his sister again," Mia explained.

Beth's mouth hardened, and she drew in a deep breath.

She understood that Mia and Hani were caught in the wheels of some gigantic impersonal machinery which would churn them up and spit them out, if it could. They were both victims of a system and that system was part of the problem.

Beth did not like systems. She liked living out in the wilds, in the middle of nowhere, helping her husband to farm the land, to raise sheep and cattle, tearing a living from the hills. She liked the struggle and the challenge, the fresh air and the freedom.

So she decided in that moment that she would let Hani and Mia complete their journey; she would give them what they needed, but she would not interfere and she would not be the one to inform the police. She was worried for their safety, but she did not think that seeing

Hani bundled off into a detention centre was necessarily the best way to keep him safe.

When they had finished eating, she took their plates away, scraped them clean into a food bin, and dipped them into the washing-up bowl full of soap suds. It gave her something to do while she thought about what to do next.

She glanced at the clock. Her husband would be back in an hour or two.

She left the radio on while she worked, and its insistent voice invaded the quiet calm of the kitchen, muttering in the background. Strains of classical music wafted until the radio presenter announced it was eleven o' clock and time for the news with Charlotte Green. A report came on, and Hani looked up when he heard the word '*Aleppo*'.

He listened intently, his face frozen, his mind travelling far away from the Scottish hills to a place that the other two in the room could not possibly imagine, a place being bombed out of existence, torn apart, its streets and buildings reduced to rubble.

"… *Reports of chlorine gas being dropped on the city of Aleppo. The injured and the wounded are too frightened to go to the hospitals which have become designated military targets for President Assad's troops… We came across this group of doctors who were trying to help those they could…*" The words cut out to the sound of a small child wailing and the reporter went on, "… *as you can hear, this is no military target…*"

Hani stopped eating.

The woman quickly reached across and switched off the radio.

There was silence for a while.

Beth leaned back against the sink, her arms folded. "I'll make up some provisions for you. Where is it you are heading?"

"We're heading for the island where my parents are from," Mia said. "We'll be safe there," she added. Hani glanced at his companion quickly, wondering why she confessed so much, when it was better to say little.

"Which island would that be?" the woman asked.

A shadow fell across Mia's face and she prevaricated. "I can't remember the name..."

Beth nodded, as if she understood.

"No need to tell me," she smiled. "A long time ago, when I was about 9, I think, I read a book called *The Children Who Lived in a Barn*."

Mia and Hani watched her, puzzled.

Beth gave a short laugh. "I always wanted to do the same, get away from everyone and live in a barn, without authorities and do-gooders fussing over you... I think that's what you're looking for and I think that's what you probably *need*, too."

She smiled sadly. "I'm just not so sure you're going to be allowed to have that. But I'll not be the one to stop you..."

She pushed away from the sink then and began to search her cupboards and fridge for packets of food they could take with them. She searched out another small rucksack, and filled that with essentials too.

Beth rattled a box of matches. "You'll need these."

She slipped in a torch as well, then she gazed sadly out of the door at the yard, and the hills beyond. She

134

frowned. She had heard something, the barking of the dogs.

"You'd best leave now," she said.

But they were too late; they heard the rumble of the trailer in the yard.

"Take yourselves off upstairs," she said hastily. "To the room at the top. On the left. No one goes in there. You'll need to stay quiet for a bit."

They did as she asked, taking everything with them – they thought.

In the room at the top of the stairs, they waited.

It was a small room with a sloping roof and a single bed, and there was evidence of a life lived within these walls that had been left behind. Nothing had been changed, it had simply been tidied.

"Her son's room," Mia whispered.

They sat on the bed and the springs creaked, then they listened to the sound of footsteps, the barking of dogs and the murmur of voices below.

They looked at each other in the silence. Could they trust this woman? What if she betrayed them?

Hani wondered for a moment if they had let their guard down too soon.

The murmuring of voices seeped up through the floorboards.

Then there was a change in the tempo.

A question being asked.

A muttered reply.

An ominous silence.

Hani began to hunt about for his sweatshirt and went cold all over when he realised he'd left it on the back of the chair.

He waited, while they listened to Beth presumably offering an explanation to her husband.

There were raised voices; shouting.

The two cowered, listening to the argument unfolding downstairs and their hearts sank.

They could not hear exactly what was being said, but one thing was clear – Beth's husband was not of the same frame of mind as his wife.

Now they were trapped.

"We should have left while we had the chance," Mia said.

THE FOREST

Slipping their backpacks on, they carefully opened the bedroom door and paused at the top of the landing.

They could hear the husband's voice carrying up the stairs.

"You've got to stop this nonsense, Beth. Michael is gone. Helping an illegal immigrant wanted by the police is not going to bring him back, or do anyone any good – least of all those kids themselves. Where are they?"

"Gregor, why do you always have to do this?"

"We're going to ring the police and tell them exactly who we've found. It's in all the papers, for Pete's sake."

"I'm doing no such thing. Why can't you just let things lie?"

"Me?" he shouted, exasperated. "I'm not the one chasing ghosts."

Into this grief-fuelled argument stepped Mia and Hani.

The man turned an angry face towards them. Hani met his unforgiving gaze; something in the bear-like man faltered. He turned away, ashamed, and in that moment, they bolted towards the door before he could think to close it.

As they escaped into the yard, they heard someone

calling them back, but they headed towards the gate. Hani could hear a bull lowing in the vast metal shed, and the wind teased his face, but when he looked up towards the far ridge he saw a sight which made him freeze on the spot: a familiar black jeep crawling its way over the bumpy gravel road towards the farm.

He stared around in panic, then he did the first thing that came into his head. The farmer's quadbike was standing idling in the yard, its trailer detached.

He leapt onto the quadbike and started the engine. Mia climbed on behind him, clinging on tightly, still clutching their two rucksacks with the precious supplies inside, while he revved it and sped out of the yard and into the fields. The black jeep was still some distance away; it hadn't yet reached the farm, but the occupants could no doubt see the quadbike heading away over the summit.

They plunged down into the next field, Hani expertly avoiding rocks and tussocks. Sheep scattered in alarm, but they kept on going and they didn't stop.

Having come so far, Hani was not about to let those men catch him without putting up a fight.

The jeep looked eerily sinister as it crept towards the farm. They had time to wonder if it was an off-road vehicle and if there were Land Rovers or other quadbikes in the farmyard which their enemies could commandeer.

But they did not pause.

Hani kept the throttle open and seared his way across the hillsides, over the next summit, with Mia clinging on, her arms wrapped round his waist.

He was tempted to turn his head to see if they were

giving chase but, afraid of losing control, he faced forward, his eyes on the ground, steering the vehicle.

Mia glanced over her shoulder, her hair flying in her face.

There was no one following them.

She turned to face the front again, smiling with relief, and leaned her cheek against Hani's back. She had never been on a quadbike before, but Hani clearly had. He steered it expertly around waiting hazards lying invisible in their path.

As Mia glanced back a second time, the jeep suddenly burst into view over the top of the last summit and came hurtling towards them.

It was still a long way off, but she felt her body go cold with fear. She clung on harder, and shouted, "They're following."

Hani opened the throttle wider and increased his speed.

He had spotted a distant woodland and was heading for the edge of this now.

When Mia risked another glance she could see that the jeep was still about a mile off.

The quadbike was making good ground, when it suddenly hit a boulder and flipped.

Mia and Hani lay winded with shock.

"This way," Hani cried.

Leaving the quadbike lying, they grabbed their backpacks and raced towards the nearby woodland. Here they entered a different world, surrounded by darkness.

A thick shadowy silence engulfed them, dense fir trees on every side. There was so little light here that all plant life was dying where the sunlight could not reach, and the ground was thick with soft brown needles.

It was dark and it was enclosed.

They pushed a way forward, crashing through branches, on and on until they were a good five hundred yards from the edge of the plantation. Then they stopped and listened. The reek of resin and pine was thick in their nostrils.

They could hear the distant rumble of an engine getting closer. It paused and they could hear car doors slamming very faintly, then voices.

Hani looked from left to right. They were surrounded by darkness, dense pine branches growing, so tightly knit that barely a creature could push between them, other than passing deer.

Then he looked upwards, where a kind of ladder presented itself in the form of branches. Up there, near the treetops, the greenery was thicker where it had not died from lack of light, and now it hid the sky from view.

He nodded at Mia, and helping each other with the first few branches, they began to climb, slowly and steadily, rung by rung, branch by branch, until they were near the top, and could no longer be seen from the ground.

Then they waited.

And they waited.

Yusuf and his men were searching the forest.

Hani could hear them crashing through the undergrowth.

They did not know it but the plantation they had entered covered a vast area, several kilometres wide. They had not had time to penetrate it very deeply, but as soon as they had stepped between the trees they were invisible, hidden from view.

Hani listened tensely. He could hear footsteps crashing along before they faded into the distance as if they'd set off in the opposite direction.

Hani and Mia remained still. They did not make the mistake of breaking cover. Here they could attempt to hide – for a while.

They heard voices, quiet footsteps, the cracking of twigs below. They did not move, hoping the greenery would hide them.

After a while, Hani glanced down. Directly beneath them, about four metres below, stood Yusuf, wearing his dull green khaki jacket, staring around like a hunter.

And next to him was a man Hani recognized from the Calais jungle; the kindly gentleman who had volunteered to help Hani and his sister. Hani remembered Uncle Giorgio's voice, his brown eyes, his silver hair, his silky-smooth promises.

"If you come with me, you will be safe. You can do some work and I will send you to school, give you homes, teach you how to live in British society."

Uncle Giorgio... with his lies and his deceit and his treacherous smile.

He was dressed in a suit, respectable as always, even as he picked his way through the undergrowth. Usually he got other men to do his dirty work for him, but this time he seemed intent on the kill.

He was a hunter.

And they were his prey.

Hani felt anger sear through his chest. He wanted to leap down, drive his fist into Uncle Giorgio's face and demand to know where they had taken his sister, but he knew it would do no good. He could not fight men like that single-handed. Mia put a calming hand on his shoulder.

They watched the men pause, look about, and move on, their footsteps slowly fading as they stealthily cracked their way through the dying undergrowth.

They were like wolves.

"It's no good," they heard Yusuf say. "They could be anywhere in here."

"Then we will comb it with a fine tooth comb," Uncle Giorgio replied.

But there was doubt in his voice, too.

The men searched for an hour, criss-crossing the plantation, combing back and forth.

Mia and Hani could hear them in the distance and in all that time they had the sense never to move. They did not panic or try to break free.

"We will come back for them in the morning," Uncle Giorgio said, his voice carrying.

Their muscles ached, they were tired and weary, but Hani and Mia let the foliage hide them. Nature was their friend and seemed to know how to keep them safe.

Mia and Hani were children of misfortune and they had learned to remain invisible. *Children should be seen and not heard*, it used to be said. But in their case, they were neither heard nor seen. They had no voice; no rights; no presence. They could vanish into thin air and no one would really care.

*

The Duke struggled in his waders across the open moorland.

He found the old ruin which he knew lay not far from where the secret tunnel ended, but there was no sign of the children.

He cursed himself for being too late. He should have set out sooner, not suffered a moment's hesitation, and then he might have caught up with them.

He stared out across the moor, aware that other men might also be staring out, wondering which route the young people had taken.

Open land as far as the eye could see and no way of knowing which way was the right way.

He pressed on.

He knew this landscape like the back of his own hand. He knew that if he headed north, up into those hills, he would be far away from other people, and he also sensed this is what Mia and Hani would want most – to be remote, hidden – but he also knew that the most experienced walkers and climbers became lost in these Scottish hills every year. Sometimes their bodies were never found, and he cursed himself again for his lack of forethought in letting them go on alone.

DARKNESS FALLS

They waited until it got dark.

There was no sign of the men; it had gone quiet long ago, and they had heard the jeep starting up again, reversing away over the rough hillside, slowly snaking a path back to the farmyard they had fled.

The quadbike was left on its side like an injured beast for the farmer, Beth's husband, to recover at his leisure. Hani felt a little guilty about this, but he'd had no choice.

"They'll be back in the morning to search properly," he told Mia.

They had not spoken in a long while and their voices were rusty.

They adjusted themselves on the branches, settling more comfortably, allowing their legs to dangle mid-air, but they were strangely reluctant to leave the safety of their treetop eyrie.

It seemed ridiculous that those men, experienced hunters as they were, had never thought to look above their heads for their human prey, to scan the upper branches. In fact, even if they had, the children would not have been visible from the ground. Lower down, the pine needles had perished and thinned through lack of light, leaving a ladder-like structure for them to climb, but up here the firs grew dense and they were lost in soft clouds of pungent greenery, fresh pine needles scenting the air and brushing their faces.

As darkness came down and the sky grew black, they slowly climbed down from their hiding place, landing on the ground with a soft thud.

The night stood still all around them, but full of night noises. Eyes seemed to stare out of the gloom, twigs cracked. It was eerie and full of threat, like some forest in a fairy tale where dangers might lurk. For these two, the dangers were real and came in human form. It reminded Mia of the fairy tale her gran used to read to her when she was little. Hansel and Gretel. She and Hani were like that, orphans lost in a wood, hiding from wicked people who wanted to do them harm. All they needed now was for a gingerbread cottage to appear in a clearing, and they would both end up roasted in an oven, while a cackling witch watched on.

In the distance they heard the pounding of hooves growing closer.

Hani grabbed the torch and shone it ahead, shouting loudly. A wild stag veered off to the right and galloped away.

"I wondered what it was," Mia cried breathlessly.

"Come on," Hani said, feeling braver now. "There is nothing to be afraid of in these woods – it's men we have to fear."

They tried to instil some confidence into one another. If the woods had been dark during daylight hours, they were intensely so now. They could see nothing ahead, even with the aid of the torch which shone a feeble light.

They edged their way forward, pushing through the undergrowth to where they judged the trees might be more sparsely planted.

Was it his imagination, or did he see figures through the trees, moving stealthily?

He switched off the torch, and listened.

Then switched it back on.

There were no figures.

It was merely the torchlight playing tricks on them.

Eventually the trees parted into a long corridor, lined with thick pines either side – an accident of planting or by design? They followed this corridor, walking along the top of a ridge which had been carved by some heavy vehicle passing through. On either side of the ridge were boggy patches and mossy stones.

Hani realised that if they kept to this corridor of trees they would eventually emerge from the forest.

It was a relief to finally break cover, out into the open.

The fields and hills stretched away from them, gently lit by moonlight.

They walked all night under the scudding clouds, shouldering their backpacks, covering as much ground as possible. Hani would not rest until they had put as much distance as possible between themselves and that farm. He glanced at his companion from time to time, wondering how fate had thrown them together.

While they walked, they munched on some dry oatcakes Mia found in the backpack Beth had thrust at them.

They avoided all roads, all signs of human habitation, and stuck to the open wilderness. If they lost themselves in an area this vast, it would be all the more difficult for Uncle Giorgio and Yusuf to find them again – so Hani reasoned.

They plunged down into a ravine, skirted along the banks for a while, and found a sheltered space beside a small burn, where it seemed safe to rest till morning.

Mia wrapped the Duke's heavy coat around them both, they finished the oatcakes and took their rest while the darkness gathered.

When the Duke arrived at the farmhouse it was already getting dark and he realised it had been a little foolish to set off on foot. He ought to have at least taken the battered old Land Rover he kept in one of the outbuildings, but he'd known there was no point. Those two young people would not stick to the roads, he knew that.

He peered across the yard and watched a woman through the lit frame of the kitchen window, an unhappy-looking woman caught unawares, gazing out at nothing, her thoughts elsewhere.

But there was movement in the yard, which made him step back smartly behind the farmyard wall. The slamming of car doors and then headlights were switched on, burning a hole in the dark. A black jeep swung out of the yard and retreated along the track.

From his hiding place, the Duke recognized the driver as one of the men who had already visited him.

He waited for the vehicle to leave, watched it crawling along the track, then went to the front door of the farmhouse and knocked.

The woman he'd seen before, framed in the window, answered it.

"I'm looking for two children," the Duke began. "I wondered if they'd been here."

She shook her head in amazement, as if life was taking her by surprise these days, and swung the door wider.

"You and the rest of the world, it seems."

"Can you help me?"

She shook her head. "They stole a quadbike and headed over that way, towards the fir plantation. Those men you saw leave just now? They couldn't find them either."

The Duke looked towards the rise of the hill and the line of trees just visible beyond. The light was fading fast now, so he nodded briefly to the woman and left.

She stood in her doorway, staring after him, thinking about the boy, Hani, and the girl with him. What were they running from, and what else could she have done to help them?

THE PAST

The past tugged at Hani and not even the presence of Mia, so warm beside him, could keep him in the present.

As he listened to the murmur of the water beside them, finding a path through the rocks, his dreams took him elsewhere…

He could feel the grey waves smacking the side of the boat…

At first, the sea seemed quite calm as they watched the coastline of Syria disappear. But he wept to be leaving his parents behind and he could hear Reena weeping too. Her arms were around him and they were surrounded on all sides by strangers, people they had never met before, although they were bound together by their troubles and the prospect of their journey.

The Mediterranean is a temperamental ocean, and its mood rapidly changed once they were a few kilometres away from the coast and into their voyage. Hani could hear a girl beside him humming to herself and he wished she would stop.

The waves rose higher, beginning to rock the boat from side to side, tipping it up at one end and down at the other. That was when the passengers on board began to wail as realisation hit home, even grown men crying out in terror, fearing they were only seconds away from certain death and a watery grave.

Hani listened to someone on his left being sick, retching hopelessly into the bottom of the boat. The stink, the effluence, the discomfort was worse than anything he had known before. Small children were crying, infants alarmed as much by the anxiety of the adults around them as by the sight of the tall grey waves pounding the sides of their flimsy vessel.

They were drenched, soaked, hungry and dirty. He and Reena had had no choice but to leave their parents behind; their parents had hoped so much that their children would be rescued from the war-torn city of Aleppo, that they would find some sort of safety and sanctuary in Europe where people would know what the Syrians were suffering.

They had planned at first to leave together as a family, but on the shore itself they were faced with a stark choice.

"*No room*," they were told. They could wait for the next boat, which may or may not be available, or they could let their children take the last two spaces on the one that was about to leave. Air strikes were imminent. The city was being constantly bombarded with barrel bombs and rockets.

They had already parted with all of their money, giving it to an organization – a man – who had promised to get people out of Syria. They had put their faith in that promise.

Hani tries not to remember the wails, the distress of his sister.

"*Mama! No!*"

The sorrow of his mother as she tore Reena's arms from around her neck.

"*No, Reena. You must go. And look after Hani for me,*" she sobbed.

How hard it must be for a mother to do that...

His mother...

The girl next to him continued to hum. There was a stir, a commotion in the middle of the boat; a woman was being passed along. Her face was pale and her body was cold. They dropped her over the side, where she slowly sank from view. All of this was done wordlessly, without comment or discussion.

Hani remembers watching her clothes briefly billow, and fill with water. He saw her glassy eyes, her face disappear and slip beneath the waves...

A LONG NIGHT...

When he opened his eyes he saw Mia staring at him.

"You were dreaming," she said.

She was pulling out supplies from the backpack Beth had given them.

It wasn't yet morning, but hunger and discomfort had put an end to their sleep for now.

"We've got water to drink," she said, gesturing at the burn which sparkled over the rocks. "And we've got food." She gazed at the two bruised bananas and two apples she'd found in the bottom of the rucksack, and frowned. "Well... sort of... Hungry?"

"Starving!"

"Let's eat now."

They were sheltered in a narrow ravine, with high walls of rock on either side where cool ferns and wet mosses clung to the stones.

Hani lit a small fire while Mia climbed down carefully in the dark and fetched water from the falls.

They sat close to the flames for warmth, ate the battered fruit and washed it down with water. Outside their circle of light they could feel the darkness of the night and all its dangers pressing on them. Hani kept glancing over his shoulder, terrified their fire would be seen.

"We'll put it out soon," Mia reassured him. "Once we're warm enough." She was secretly impressed by his fire-lighting skills and wondered how much practice he'd had back in his hometown when electricity and power were scarce.

"When we get to the island," she said softly, "you'll see how beautiful it is."

Hani said nothing.

"There's the sea, and the beaches," she went on.

"We have to cross the sea to get there?" he said suddenly, lifting his head.

"'Course! It's an island."

"I don't like the sea."

Mia looked at him, and smiled.

"Don't worry. We'll find your sister first," she added.

"You cannot promise that," and she knew he was right, but she was doing her best to be cheerful.

"That woman was nice," she said thoughtfully. "Beth."

He nodded, frowning. "That book she read when she was a child..." He added, "What did she mean? *The Children Who Lived in a Barn*?"

"I suppose she meant it was a bit like us. Surviving. Without adults. In a place you wouldn't expect."

He looked up at the sky. "In Aleppo I spent all my time looking up at the skies – not at the stars or the moon or the clouds. We were looking out for barrel bombs."

Mia stared at him.

He had never really talked about his life before, and she wanted to know more. She had heard stuff about the war in Syria on the radio and the news, snippets which were forever cropping up, but she didn't really understand.

"What was it like?" she asked now.

He paused, gazing out at the hills, and his gaze seemed to disappear to another time and place in his mind where Mia could not follow.

"There were concrete shelters, without food or toilets or running water, nothing but a corridor of rooms with, here and there, an old mattress to sit on, while we would wait in the dark and listen to the crump of the explosions getting closer."

There was a slight pause and Mia couldn't help thinking that the murmur of the burn beside them and the peaceful moor beyond seemed such a far cry from the world that her new friend was describing.

"The White Helmet Corps: my uncle was a member of that. When he put on his white helmet, it was his job to rescue the injured from the rubble... once the dust had cleared. My cousin was an ambulance driver, a very dangerous job."

She waited for him to go on; she avoided interrupting him and so he talked on, more than he had ever talked before.

"Me and Reena, when we were working in that factory, in those sheds, we heard there are no hospitals left in Aleppo. They have all been bombed. One half of the city is under siege. There are only 32 doctors left to cope with the people who are badly injured... or dying. Sometimes we set fire to tyres on the streets near our home, in the hope that the black smoke would hide us from the air. It never worked. One crazy man fought back with balloons – our neighbour. He filled them full of gas, put nails on the end and sent them up into the sky. He said they would stay up there for 15 hours and the nails would destroy the engines of those planes. Crazy man... Of course, it never worked."

"They would drop barrels full of explosives from airplanes above our heads. But they always dropped them in twos, so that once you heard one explosion you knew that another was sure to follow. We would see a black cloud a few streets away, smoke rising, and people would come out onto the street to stare, and rush to the place to help, knowing they were the lucky ones that time."

"We were frightened all the time – tired. All the children had big dark shadows under their eyes. My mother's school was bombed, so she took in children in the cellar of the building where we lived and tried to teach them there. Even in the nursery they knew all about death and bombs and shelling. They knew life was fragile and that you could be snatched away in moments, but if you asked any of them if they were afraid of the airplanes that flew overhead they said 'No!' and smiled with bravery."

Hani fell silent, and tears slid down his face. "I miss my city, I miss Aleppo."

Mia said nothing. She simply listened.

"No one here understands what it was like. Our parents sent us away to safety while they had the chance. Now people are stuck in the part of the city where we lived and cannot get out. But my mother and father did not know they were sending me to this. They thought that people here would help us."

She was silent, lost for words.

"But the only person who has really helped me…" he turned to look at her, "is you."

She coughed slightly and shuffled her feet, felt herself blushing. She was never very good at emotion – so she thought.

"You've helped me too," she admitted roughly.

"How?"

"My life is better now."

"Yes, now you have the whole world chasing after you. Is that good?"

She shrugged. "Yes, it's good. Before, I had no one."

Mia and Hani shared a similar longing, for home and safety, somewhere they could call their own. That was what Angie and Clifford had been supposed to offer – in the eyes of the council and other authorities – but somehow, the reality had not quite worked out that way. Mia thought of the massive widescreen TV which took up most of the living room wall; she thought of the extension being built, the ugly little conservatory where the kids could 'hang out.' Mia had been their only foster child at the time, but they had plans to make room for many more. It brought them an income. Oh, they ticked all the right boxes, of course, made sure they satisfied the authorities. They knew the rules, how it worked. They played the system, and it brought a steady income while at the same time they were seen to be caring for waifs and strays. But there was no love there – no warmth, no proper care or bonding. Nothing but food on a plate, the right questions being asked at the right time of day, a patronizing heartless veneer that never fooled Mia – and others like her – for one moment.

"Why were you unhappy with Angie and Clifford?" he asked now.

She shrugged. "I just was."

"You had food and warmth. You had a bed."

"And no love. I felt like a stranger in their house. It wasn't my home."

"I understand."

"If a foster child is unhappy and kicks up a fuss," she said, thinking out loud, "you get moved on and they note it down in your file." She put on a professional-sounding voice, "They say *relations have broken down*. I didn't do any of that stuff. I didn't shout or make trouble for anyone. That's not my style, to cause a scene."

Hani nodded. He could believe it. In the short time he'd known her, he could see that Mia was not the sort to noisily demand attention.

All she had done was run away because she was deeply unhappy and wanted to find something of what she had lost...

She might not find what she was looking for on the island, but surely it was her right to try?

THE VOICE

Hours passed and the children slept a little more in the early dawn, cold and exhausted.

Then something strange filtered through into Hani's dreams, making him twitch and stir in his sleep, warning him of danger approaching.

He sat up, his shoulders tense, wondering what it was he'd just heard.

He'd heard a sound carrying clearly across the moor. It sounded eerie, ghoulish even, like a lost soul, and it was coming from the direction they'd travelled in.

He held himself erect, listening with every muscle in his body.

There it came again, drifting on the breeze, a soft haunting call.

A human voice.

And again.

"Hallooo…?" A fleeting echo, thin on the air.

He and Mia listened, blinking in the dark, wondering if they'd imagined it.

"What the…?" Mia murmured.

It kept repeating itself, and grew nearer. And nearer.

Hani stood up and peered out across the moor. Then he thought he heard his own name.

A very faint echo of itself on the night air.

"Hallooo? Hani?"

His eyes grew wide in the dark, and then at last a figure came into view, a distant black smudge on the horizon. It was hard to see if it was human at first, but it appeared to detach itself from the shapes around it, and was moving not towards them exactly, but off on a trajectory to the right.

And it kept on stubbornly calling out Hani's name.

He froze.

Not a ghost then, or a ghoul, but a human in search of its prey.

He ducked down.

But would Yusuf or Uncle Giorgio call out his name like that?

Most definitely they would, so Hani remained still.

If they made a move it would reveal their whereabouts. Best to keep schtum.

They watched as the lone figure drifted off to the right, missing its target. If they kept very still then the intruder would move on and miss them entirely. All they needed to do was stay quiet.

Then a doubt entered Mia's mind.

It was a lone figure, with a wide-brimmed hat by the look of things, and was that fishing gear protruding from its back? Would Yusuf or Uncle Giorgio really act like that? This person did not seem to fit the description or behaviour of the men who had pursued them in the black jeep, but it did fit the description of a certain kindly old gentleman they had encountered the day before last.

Mia leapt up, and before she knew it she had switched on the torch and was waving it in the air.

"Hello?" she called out bravely, aware of the risk she was taking. "We're over here."

"What are you doing?"

Hani tried to grab her arm, but she continued to wave the torch in the air.

The shape stopped, turned and began to move slowly in their direction.

For a moment or two Mia wondered if she'd made a mistake, but all doubt vanished when a familiar voice cried out in an absurdly friendly tone, "Ah! Here you are! At last! I thought I'd never see you again."

Smiling with relief, the Duke beamed down at them. "My goodness, what a trek I've had. And what a fuss you're causing."

He regarded them both and smiled. "Don't worry. Don't be frightened. I'm not going to shop you to the authorities. Can't be doing with the blasted lot of them myself. I thought you might need a spot of help."

Mia and Hani gazed at him as if they couldn't believe their eyes. However, Hani couldn't help remembering another apparently well-meaning gentleman he had once trusted in the Calais jungle, and wondered if his luck was to be believed.

THE DUKE

"Look here, you two," he began. "I felt awfully wretched letting you wander off by yourselves like that, without anyone to help."

He opened his arms wide.

"So, here I am." He looked down at the remains of their fire. "Room for a littlun?"

Hani peered over the Duke's shoulder to check there was no one following him, or lurking behind.

"You're on your own?" Mia said.

A shadow of sadness passed across the Duke's face as he reassured them that yes, he was most definitely on his own.

"You promise?"

"I came across a farmhouse way over in that direction and encountered your friends in the jeep again."

Hani tensed nervously but the Duke went on. "It's okay. They didn't see me at all. They didn't have a clue I was there. Stupid old fool came on foot, didn't I?"

"How on earth did you find us?"

He grinned, obviously pleased with himself.

"I have my skills. I've been roaming this countryside since I was a boy. I know a thing or two about how to cope out here, how to read the signs."

"Like a Native American?" Mia cried, unable to conceal the relief and delight she felt.

"Mmm… sort of. Anyway, how's tricks?"

Both of them looked confused, and Mia wondered for a moment if he was under the mistaken impression they had a dog called Tricks with them.

"It's just an expression," he laughed.

"Now, we've got some serious walking to do."

"Where to?"

"Well, back to Greystone Hall for one thing, before we set about making a few more plans and an itinerary."

"Greystone Hall?"

"My house, you remember? I've got an old Land Rover there which will cover a good deal more distance than us on foot. We have a mission to accomplish."

Mia grinned. It was clear he was enjoying the adventure, as if he saw himself as some kind of leisurely and aged James Bond, out to defeat the baddies.

She liked the idea too, and was more than happy to fall in with his plans.

"Now then, now then," he clapped his hands together smartly, like a sergeant major. "We have a long trek ahead of us, so let's get started."

Hani followed, but still he felt uneasy in his mind.

Having been through so much, it was hard to trust any adult who promised to help.

GREYSTONE HALL

It was indeed a long trek back to the Duke's mansion, concealed behind its belt of trees, but the old gentleman was as good as his word and knew exactly the quickest route to get there.

It was several hours later that they stumbled through the front door and into the vast interior of the stone-flagged hallway. The house was as they had left it: quiet, barely inhabited, rooms full of books, empty fireplaces, old family heirlooms hanging discreetly on the walls or accumulating dust in the corners.

The Duke ushered them into the vast room on the first floor where they had first encountered him. He crouched before the fireplace and set about lighting a fire.

"Now then," he said, "You two settle yourselves down on couches here, make yourselves comfortable. It's better you sleep here. Warmer. Then we'll talk again in the morning. You need some rest first."

He drew the door behind him and left them both to their slumbers. Mia couldn't sleep. She stared around inquisitively at the room which to her seemed like a museum, to show how the landed gentry lived.

"What if those men turn up again?" Hani asked the Duke before he left them.

"Then we hide you somewhere about the place. And this time, we wait for them to leave first."

The next morning he gave them breakfast and unfolded a map of the Highlands and Islands, smoothing it across the table.

"So... Balnakeil Bay you say?"

"That's right," Hani said. "That's where I believe they have taken my sister. We think they might be keeping her in a house there..."

"*Balfour House*!" Mia added.

"Okay, well I can drive you as far as Tongue. As it happens, a friend of mine lives in a craft village not far from there. You know," he added "I can contact people in the Government if you want. Get them to do something... it's easily done."

"No!" Hani shook his head, fear starting in his eyes, and Mia added her voice to his. "We don't want the authorities getting involved. It will only lead to more trouble."

The Duke acquiesced, although reluctantly. After all they had been through, he could see their point only too clearly, and shared their distrust. The likelihood was that if he got anyone else involved, cogs would begin turning and Mia would be returning to her foster parents within the hour. He could understand how that might not feel like such a wonderful prospect for her. If he could help these two find Hani's sister whilst evading the many people who were after them – both do-gooders and traffickers – then he would.

BALNAKEIL BAY

They had driven most of the morning in the Duke's battered Land Rover when they noticed the landscape changing. They could smell the ocean long before they saw it. The air seemed lighter, the land more open. It felt as if they were closer to the sky somehow.

It was around noon when they spotted a cluster of grey barrack-like buildings ahead, and a sign marked with the words Balnakeil Craft Village.

The Duke stopped the Land Rover and peered round at them.

"That's it. That's the village where Luca Toft – God love her – has lived for more than thirty years. Strange place," he murmured.

Mia peered through the windscreen at the small huts hunkering down among the grasses. Some of them were painted with brightly-coloured flowers on the exterior walls in an attempt to prettify them.

It looked a bleak spot to live in, the grey of sea and sky surrounding it, the grey of the buildings, utilitarian structures built with ugly concrete breeze blocks.

"Used to be an early warning air raid station in the Fifties," he explained, "but they decommissioned it during the Cold War – realised it wouldn't make a bloody bit of difference in the end, if we were all intent on blowing each other to Kingdom Come, so they sold the bunkers to a group of artists in search of cheap accommodation, who promptly set about sprucing the place up a bit. Luca loves it here, painted her bunker all the colours of the rainbow, God love her. Mad as a broom, of course."

They were silent, gazing around them at the strange little village inhabited by artists, their pots and flowers neatly arranged outside, where they cowered out of the wind.

"And that, my friends," he pointed across the bay to a distant structure which stood out stark against the landscape "must be *Balfour House*!"

It loomed across the bay, within reach at last.

Hani stared.

After all this time, they were within sight of it. He wanted to race across that beach and batter the door down, search every room before it was too late, but at the same time he was afraid of what he might find. The Duke held him back.

"There's no point in rushing ahead. It won't serve any purpose."

They parked the Land Rover at the bay and peered across the sand dunes.

The Duke took out a pair of binoculars and trained them on *Balfour House*, then passed them first to Hani.

"That's them, look," the Duke muttered, pointing. "The same black jeep parked outside."

It sat there in the dusky light like a beetle, sinister and dark, but there was no sign of Yusuf or Uncle Giorgio.

"So," the Duke sighed, "We need to exercise caution.

First things first, do you know what would be an excellent idea? To speak to someone local who knows the place, and what better person than Luca herself? I propose we drive back to the village and speak to her. The more people who know we're here, the better. I know what you're thinking, but believe me, Luca is not the busybody type. She's no friend of the authorities either, I can assure you."

Hani did not move. He sat staring across the bay, his eyes fixed upon the stark outline of that house, and then out to a distant spot where a small yacht sat moored out to sea. He could not explain it, but his eyes were drawn there, as if by a magnet.

"I can't leave here," he muttered.

"Sorry?"

"I can't leave this spot. Someone needs to keep an eye on the place, make sure we don't miss any movement."

"I'm not sure that..." the Duke began.

"Leave me here with the binoculars and I'll hide in the grasses and wait till you get back."

The Duke hesitated, unsure.

"I'll stay with him," Mia said.

"Well... you'll need to promise me you won't do anything stupid?"

"We won't budge from this spot."

The Duke sighed heavily.

"I'll leave these with you, but promise me you will not move. Understand?"

"Promise!" Mia repeated.

"Hani?" the Duke pressed.

Hani gave a brief nod.

A few minutes later they watched the battered old

Land Rover trundle away, their old friend, the Duke, at the wheel, and settled themselves down in the dip of a sand dune to watch the house.

Hani lay with the binoculars pressed to his eyes and his gaze never faltered.

A soft breeze blew through the grasses and whistled across the sand. They were in for a long vigil.

BALFOUR HOUSE

The house reared up before them, stark on the skyline; familiar from the screenshot they had seen when Mia still had her phone.

They had travelled halfway across Scotland for this: the sea stretched away to their left, and now they were within sight. It rose above the sand dunes, dirty-yellow in the light, with tiny narrow windows like a prison. It had a sloping grey roof with four tall chimney stacks. The gable end was perpendicular to the beach and the ferocious winds which would hurtle off the Atlantic.

Balfour House sat with its back to the sea for a reason. It was obdurate, unapproachable, with a hint of institutionalized deprivation about it.

It was hard to imagine who might live here – if anyone did.

Its windows were blank, narrow and barred. They were also positioned high up in the walls so it was impossible to see within. *Balfour House* was a closed mystery.

The setting sun caught the angles of the yellow-white walls and bathed them gold.

There was no movement of any kind that they could see, no human presence, no lights within.

"Get down!" Hani whispered suddenly.

They crouched low, flat against the side of the dune.

Three men emerged from the side of the house and while the other two climbed into the jeep, one of them stopped and stood gazing out to sea.

Hani tensed and Mia could hear his breathing next to her. He had recognized Uncle Giorgio. It seemed impossible that the one man they had spent the past few days avoiding should be here now, within a few hundred metres of where they lay.

Hani could have avoided him forever. Instead, he was deliberately seeking him out; the most dangerous man in the Calais jungle. One of them, anyway... The world was full of monsters who came in human disguise. This was something Hani had learned in his short life.

He had sought out his old enemy, tracked him down to this remote and windswept spot on the north-west coast of Scotland because it was the one place where he hoped to have sight of his sister, Reena.

Uncle Giorgio finally climbed into the jeep with the others, reversed it back along the track, then drove away.

Hani made to stand up, but Mia stopped him with a hand on his arm. "Wait. We promised the Duke!"

"You think I can let this opportunity slip? It's now or never. Reena could be in that building somewhere."

No one was going to stop him from going to her right this instant.

Mia watched in despair as he ran forward across the sand dunes. Reluctantly, she followed.

*

They could hear the tide hissing on the sand below and a stiff sea breeze blew through the marram grass. No sound carried across to them from the front of *Balfour House*.

When Uncle Giorgio had appeared, it had looked as if he was glancing in their direction.

Hani recalled the moment he first set eyes on that man, appearing through the lanes of mud between the canvas tents, like a devil in disguise, walking the earth without permission.

He'd still not lost his sense of betrayal. He and Reena had felt cheated, foolish almost for having believed his promises.

Then – once they were installed in the factory farm in the middle of nowhere – they had never seen Uncle Giorgio again. He had disappeared from their radar to be replaced by men like Yusuf.

Until now...

They watched the infamous black jeep rumble slowly away over the uneven tracks towards the tarmac road above.

This was Hani's chance and he had to grab it.

BREAKING AND ENTERING

Hani ran low against the side of the house, its walls looming over them like a fortress. Mia, following him, could feel her backpack bouncing lightly on her back, and she kept her head down, bent over slightly, copying Hani.

There were no windows at their level. All of them were too high to reach, so they edged their way around the far corner, away from the beach. Suddenly it was quieter, sheltered from the wind.

There were no other vehicles nearby.

A great heavy door faced away from the Atlantic, on purpose no doubt. The house had been built with the climate and position in mind. It was a plain house, but it had a stark presence, a closed personality about it, lurking there against the storms, giving nothing away.

The entrance at the back had a doorpiece with a date and an inscription on it.

1727 MMD

God Sees You

It was a strange inscription to have and for a moment Hani wondered what it meant. *God sees you...* He sees your actions? Was that true? Did he see what Uncle

Giorgio and men like him were capable of? Did he see the bombing and the shelling in Hani's city of Aleppo, where children were suffering and dying? And if so, if God *did* see, why did he do nothing?

All these thoughts passed through Hani's brain in a flash, as he examined the entrance to the mysterious *Balfour House* and worked out what to do next.

The door was thick and wooden, and it was padlocked.

He rattled the padlock. There was no way it would yield. In desperation he bent and picked up a stone. Mia watched him in silence, wondering what he would do, until he began to hammer the padlock with it, but it was no use. It made no impact.

"Shush," she cried. "Someone will hear."

"Do you think I care?" he rounded on her. "I want everyone to hear. My sister is in there."

Mia grasped his wrist.

"I know that, but you need to make less noise. What if there's someone else in there – one of them?"

"There's no one guarding it now," Hani said. "Otherwise, why would they have padlocked it from the outside?"

Despite Hani's efforts, the huge door with its solemn inscription was impenetrable, but meanwhile Mia had begun to edge along the wall towards a window on the ground floor at the back.

"Hey," she called. "Come here."

There were wooden boards nailed across it.

Hani, still clutching the sharp stone he'd grabbed, began to insert one edge between the boards and levered it until it splintered slightly. He worked away, Mia helping him, until one of the boards came free, and they cast it down on the grass, then clambered over the ledge through the windowless frame.

They landed with a thud in an empty drawing room, with some signs of occupation. There were mattresses on the floor, a fireplace where there was evidence of burnt paper and ash.

Their footsteps echoed through the hollow room, quietly resounding in the emptiness. It was a strange place, full of ghosts, former lives lived and then abandoned.

"Reena?" Hani heard his own voice echo, but no one answered him. Not his sister, or anyone else.

They crossed into the hall and gazed up at a wide staircase, spiralling up to the floors above. One of the windows high up was broken. Suddenly there was a screech and a trapped magpie flapped towards them, its iridescent plumage black and monstrous in the half-light.

It came to rest on the banister above and peered at them, watching.

Mia put her foot on the bottom stair, but Hani stopped her. "Careful. You don't know they're safe."

He was right, the building was in bad repair. Rain had got in through the leaking roof so they had to pick their way carefully, listening out for rotted floorboards. Hani knew about dangerous buildings, and when a stairway might be near to collapse. He tested the bottom stair first, then kept to the side. Mia followed him.

They crept up the staircase, checking the rooms on the floor above. Doors stood empty onto a desolate sight: fireplaces, abandoned bedframes, mattresses, the odd chair, but nothing else. The walls, once grand, were streaked with damp and peeling where the plaster had fallen off in long crumbling chunks.

As each room revealed its secrets, Hani's disappointment grew. There was no sign here of his sister, Reena.

There was evidence that people had been here recently though – the mattresses, the used fireplaces, a camping stove set up in one of the downstairs rooms, with cooking pots and tins nearby – but of his sister there was no sign.

"She's been here, I know it," he said.

Mia watched him, her heart sore for him. There was nothing she could say, no words of comfort she could offer.

On the top floor Hani sank down onto his haunches against the wall, then stretched his legs out in front of him in an attitude of despair.

"You can't give up," Mia said, watching him.

"I'm not. I'm thinking."

He pulled his knees up towards him, hid his face in his arms.

Mia had not seen him look this vulnerable before, like a small child left alone and abandoned, as if he had given up hoping. He was hiding the tears and the pain he was feeling.

She thought how childlike his gestures suddenly seemed, his body curling in on itself, and her heart ached for him.

He flung a fist down beside him and swept the dusty floorboards with his bare knuckles. "What's the use? I'll never find her."

He thought of his sister's smile, her reassurance, her

calm brown eyes. She had looked after him, cared for him – just as their mother had asked her to. For six months they had lain on a dirty old mattress in a metal shed on the factory farm, and she had put her arms around him at night so that he felt warm and safe, despite the terrible circumstances they'd found themselves in. She had stood beside him at their workbench as they slid the carrots towards them over the cold blade, crate after crate, hour after hour, until exhaustion left them drained of energy.

She had watched over him, giving him advice, warning him when to keep his head down.

And now she was gone, and with the best will in the world, Mia could not help him find his sister again.

The reality of his loss sank in. It was as though – in locating *Balfour House* and finding it empty – he had lost his final hope. He had been grasping at straws, trying to keep his hope alive.

Mia so wanted to help him, but how could she?

She looked around the room in desperation, feeling completely out of her depth. What could she do?

The answer came to her in the silence.

Nothing…

There was nothing she could do.

There was no race she could run to win this battle.

All she could do was stay with him.

So that's what she did.

She didn't try to make things seem better than they were. She sat with him a while, letting him feel whatever it was he needed to feel. Most of what Hani had gone through was way beyond Mia's experience.

She could not possibly imagine what it felt like to

have your city bombed, to see your schoolfriends perish around you, to leave your parents behind while they made the sacrifice of sending you halfway across the continent on a makeshift boat that was inadequate to cope with the rough seas. And what must life in Aleppo have been like, if they were willing to risk ocean storms rather than stay behind in the rubble and watch their city being pounded to obliteration around them?

No, Mia could not imagine any of that: what it felt like to cling to a boat through a night of storms, hoping to see land, seeing other people drown, and then, once land was sighted, being greeted by a perilous truck journey through a hostile Europe that did not want to see your face there, and then into the muddy desolation of the Calais jungle. A poverty trap, which Hani and Reena had fled from with the 'protection' of Uncle Giorgio. And then the factory farms, and the carrot-topping sheds, and the empty fields with no sign posts, the glinting polytunnels with subdued young people working away mysteriously in both the heat and the cold, hidden from view so that not even a helicopter or satellite could glimpse their presence. They were a hidden army of migrant workers, invisible people, slaving away for nothing more than a plate of food and a mattress to sleep on.

Without passport or papers. Without status.

Hani simply did not exist.

Mia could not imagine any of that.

But she could imagine losing your family and being forced to go to places where you did not want to be, with people you did not really want to be with. She knew what it meant to be lonely and orphaned, to have no friends, no thought of a future to look forward to because there was no Mum or Dad to applaud her on her journey, to cheer at her little triumphs.

There was no one.

She was carrying only one passenger on her own personal journey and that was herself.

Hani was the same.

The Duke could not help them. No one could. With the best will in the world, there was nothing even a wealthy man like he could do.

Mia rose and crossed to the window, stood looking out at the distant fields under the fading light. She could see the machair blowing in the breeze, a sprinkling of wildflowers, and tufts of bog cotton trembling like lambs' tails – wispy, as if left there by accident and caught on the grasses.

She knew it was called the machair because she remembered from her days spent on the island with her parents. It was protected land, wildflowers which needed to be saved from the corrosion caused by cars and tourists and walkers tramping the flowers underfoot.

Her gaze focussed on the far road, towards the village of breeze block bunkers where the Duke was seeking out his friend, Luca.

She straightened up, peered closer.

Her eye was caught by movement on the horizon, the sight of two beady headlights approaching through the gloom.

Her whole body quivered with tension as she realised

what she was looking at: the return of the shiny black jeep, with Hani's enemies inside it.

She spun round.

"Quick, Hani. We need to move."

He was still lost in his thoughts of Reena and his disappointment at not finding her here.

He looked up at Mia, his gaze empty.

"They're coming back," she hissed, and at last he realised what she was trying to say. Scrambling upright, they raced from the room and pounded down the stairs, forgetting to check for rotten floorboards. The magpie screamed in protest and set up a clattering racket, flapping around the high walls of the hallway.

They flew through the dark house, Mia in the lead. Her heels had sprouted wings again, just as they always did. She could fly when she wanted to.

They shot into the large drawing room. The window ledge was higher to climb from the inside, the floor being sunken slightly, so they had to help each other over the sill and then drop down onto the grass beneath.

There would be no hiding the damage to the wooden board they had ripped away from the window in gaining entry to the building.

They could hear the car pulling up on the grassy verge, then voices as the men began to make their leisurely way to the back of the house which faced away from the beach.

Hani and Mia pressed themselves flat against the wall, keeping low, edging their way one step ahead of their enemies whose voices they could hear approaching. The men went to the door, began to unlock the padlock, pulling at the chains. Mia and Hani could hear all of this from where they stood, pressed against the corner of the gable, listening. Then they heard the modulation in the voices change. One of the men had spotted the damage to the window and there was an ominous silence as they gathered round to inspect it.

Hani held his breath. He could feel Mia beside him, ready to run.

It wouldn't be long before Yusuf and his men would explore around this side of the house.

Hani thought of the Duke and hoped against hope he would return before it was too late.

He spun around, looking for somewhere to hide, but realised the inevitable truth – there was nowhere. They would need to make a run for it.

Reading his thoughts, Mia broke away from the house, pulling Hani with her, and headed off towards the beach across the reedy dunes, kicking up sand behind them, their feet pounding, their hearts thudding. If they could just get far enough away and... they landed with a thump into the dip of a dune and waited a moment.

"Did they see us?"

"I don't think so."

It was no longer full daylight. The sinking sun had leached light from the shoreline and the hills, so maybe they hadn't been noticed.

Mia half rose, and glanced behind her.

What she saw made her reach for Hani and pull him to his feet.

Yusuf had spotted them and was hard on their heels, sprinting through the sand dunes.

She could hear gulls screeching above their heads, the wind in their ears, the sea lashing the shoreline.

She wanted to run like the wind, take off like she used to in the stadium in Grangefield, when she went there to train in the mornings before school. She wanted to break away and fly, leaving everything behind, but she couldn't because she needed to hang onto Hani, and he was tired and couldn't run as fast as Mia. She couldn't leave him behind, but he had lost his edge, his hope, she could feel it.

It was difficult to run through the sand, up and down the dunes, but Yusuf was finding it difficult too. She could hear the huff of his breath, but then she saw something else out of the corner of her eye.

Another figure was tearing along the flat sand of the beach to her left, heading them off, like a wolf. They were closing in on their prey, hunting she and Hani down like the helpless creatures they were.

There was no one to stop them, no one to witness this chase to the death. The beach was empty. The sea curled in on the sand, wiping away the footsteps of the one solitary dog-walker who had passed this way earlier.

As she heard Hani cry out behind her, she thought fleetingly of the Duke and how sorry she was they had broken their promise to him. And in the same instant she turned, distraught, to see Hani cowering away from Yusuf's grasp. The man he had always feared, who had silently terrorized him in the carrot-topping shed with his calm insistence that Hani could do better, and if he did not do better, then he would be disposed of, peremptorily, without any thought of guilt or responsibility. These men were morally redundant; nothing disturbed them. They looked at the small and vulnerable people who came into their domain, and they saw them not as people but as goods; to be bought and sold, to be bartered for, used and then disposed of when they were no longer needed, when they had ceased to perform effectively. They treated workers as they would treat farm animals. Merchandise without feelings. Hani knew this, even if Mia did not.

As Yusuf grabbed hold of the boy and the two looked into each other's eyes again, Hani remembered that silent gesture Yusuf had made when he had cut his hand open on the blade and it had bled.

"What will I do with you if you cannot work?" he had said, almost gently.

Then he had lifted a forefinger to his own temple and pretended to fire a pistol.

Nothing had terrified Hani more than that silent gesture. When the man had spoken with such gentleness at first, he had mistakenly thought he cared, only to realise the opposite was true. This man had no scruples. He could discard Hani and his sister as easily as throwing away the scraps of his breakfast, left uneaten.

Mia stopped running.

She gave up.

She could not leave Hani to his fate.

The wolves had closed upon him and brought him down…

CAPTURED

Hani lay on his side in the darkness, his sister beside him. His head ached and he was weary to the point of exhaustion. Dark thoughts clouded his mind, but Reena was beside him. He reached out a hand in the dark and touched soft cloth, a small wiry shoulder, tight with tension.

He opened his eyes wider.

The person beside him moved.

He sat up.

Then he remembered.

His friend Mia lay beside him.

Disappointment flooded him, and then guilt that he should feel like this after his new friend had stood by him throughout everything.

He remembered tearing through the dunes, struggling against the downward pull of the sand like wading through water. They had closed around him – Yusuf and Karl – cutting off his retreat, wearing him down like a pack of wolves with their prey, and he also remembered that Mia could have run on if she'd wanted to. She had been free to keep going, far away from their clutches. She could truly run like the wind, faster than anyone Hani had ever seen, but she could not bear to leave him behind in the power of Yusuf and his friends.

She had allowed herself to be captured when she could have escaped. She had made that sacrifice for him.

And now she was here in the dark with him, waiting to be 'dealt with'.

How could he feel disappointed that it was Mia beside him and not his sister Reena?

Then despair flooded him as he realised the truth.

Reena was gone.

Perhaps he would never see her again.

Perhaps it would not be possible to trace her, and his heart clenched at the thought that she might just be a body somewhere, and that no one would care.

But he had to pull back from these dark thoughts otherwise there would be no point in continuing.

He had to stay strong. For Reena's sake. It was what she would want.

As they'd been escorted back into the abandoned entrance of Balfour House he had glanced up again at the inscription above the door.

God Sees You…

He recalled it now.

He sees what you do, Hani whispered, thinking of Yusuf and Uncle Giorgio. *He sees what you do, and he sees what you have done. And he sees me. He does not forget I am here.*

Mia turned her head.

She could hear Hani whispering beside her, and she

184

reached out a hand in the dark and clutched his.

"It's okay, Hani," she said quietly. "I'm here."

He blinked his eyes in the gloom. "We didn't find Reena," he whispered.

"No, we didn't," she said slowly.

"We tried though, didn't we?"

"We tried very hard," Mia said softly. She felt as if her heart was breaking for him, but she tried not to let it show. "But we haven't given up trying."

"No," he murmured, "we haven't given up."

There was a comfort to be had in repeating her words back to her. Like a mantra; as if somehow it was a spell which could break their torment, deliver them to freedom.

"Where are we?" he asked.

"We're in the basement of the house," Mia said. "Don't you remember? They took us down those steps – into the cellar?"

Hani nodded, his mind still confused.

He remembered now. The cold and the damp, the fear as Yusuf and Karl pushed them down those greasy stairs, treacherous underfoot. Hani had stumbled and slipped on the bottom stair, but they had laughed and pushed him regardless, then clamped the cellar door shut behind them, plunging them into darkness.

"You could have got away," Hani whispered.

Mia said nothing.

"You didn't have to stay. You could have been on the road, made your way back to the Duke."

Mia didn't voice her next thought. It was true. She could have escaped and fetched help, but instead she'd decided to stay with Hani. How stupid was she?

Hani seemed to be reading her mind and murmured, "Don't worry. He'll come and find us, I'm sure."

But right now, neither of them felt sure of anything.

How could they even trust the Duke?

Who was he, after all? And why was he so keen to help them?

The walls were running with damp. The men had taken Mia's backpack and her few precious belongings with it – the pebbles collected on the island all those years ago and which she had always kept with her.

She slumped against the floor but something dug into her hip. She felt in her pocket, and pulled out the torch Beth had given them, shone it around the walls. It was a dismal space and the floor seemed to be polluted with foetid puddles, but Hani let out such a yelp that she turned to him, panicked.

In the brief flash of light, he had seen something, a glint of purple silk in the gloom.

"The torch!" he cried, and took it from her. As he shone its beam into a dark corner of the cellar, the light picked out a lilac scarf, lying muddied and torn in the wet. It was painfully familiar to him. Hani lifted it, held it to his face.

"It's hers."

He glanced at Mia. "This is my sister's. It belongs to her. It means she has been here."

He held the silk to his nose, breathed in her familiar scent and felt a burst of hope, knowing she had been here before him; perhaps he had missed her only by minutes or hours.

He met Mia's gaze then and added sadly, "But she's not here now."

"But this is a good thing," she insisted. "It means we're very close."

"But how close?"

Mia shrugged, and as she glanced around the damp cellar she shuddered at the thought of what might have happened to Reena. But she had to hide her fears from Hani. She had to keep him strong; she had to encourage him to keep fighting and not give up hope of finding Reena, otherwise they would both be sucked under and never find a way out.

She thought of the times she had sat watching television with Angie and Clifford; news items of a missing person, and the police always stated that when an item of clothing was found it was a bad sign. It meant the owner of it was no longer alive.

She switched off the flashlight to spare the battery.

"Reena wouldn't have liked it in here."

She heard Hani's small hopeless voice in the darkness.

"Don't worry, Hani. We'll find her."

They could hear the sound of movement up above, footsteps crossing heavily, despite the thickness of the floor. They could hear laughter, and again Hani was struck by the awful irony that men like that – capable of such evil – were able to laugh and tell jokes while they were in the process of destroying lives. It seemed incredible. It was not what he had been taught to believe about human beings. Adults were supposed to be there to offer guidance and support but both Hani and Mia had learnt very quickly in their short lives that sometimes the opposite is true.

The Duke would have returned to the sand dune

where he'd left them by now, and found them missing. What would he do?

"He won't leave us here. He'll barge into the house," Mia said.

"How can he, all on his own? Those men are dangerous."

"Then he'll get the police."

"We made him promise not to."

"There are some promises it's okay to break, and I'm sure he knows that too."

But Hani did not voice his other suspicion. He still wasn't sure they could trust the Duke any more than he should have trusted Uncle Giorgio.

Mia flicked the flashlight on again and searched the grimy cellar.

"How long ago do you think she was here?" she asked softly.

"I don't know. It still has her smell," and at the thought he was hit by such a forlorn rush of longing it almost floored him.

LUCA TOFT

The Duke was in two minds about leaving them in the sand dunes within sight of *Balfour House*, but they were utterly determined. Who could blame them after everything they'd been through?

He drove on to Balnakeil Craft Village and sought out his friend Luca's hut, going over in his head how he would go about explaining the details of his story to her.

Thankfully, Luca was the type who didn't really ask for explanations and he knew she would see the truth of it all.

He parked the Land Rover and made his way down the narrow path to a painted bunker with a patio of garden pots at the front of it. He knocked on the door and waited.

It hadn't occurred to him that Luca might not be at home. He peered through the windows, but the little hut was in darkness. He stood gazing about, wondering what to do.

Of course, nothing went unnoticed in a tiny community like this, so when one of Luca's neighbours appeared, the Duke was glad to ask for help.

They asked him inside, and he sat with them over a pot of tea.

"She shouldn't be all that long. Luca loves a storm, you see, and going out in one."

"A storm?" the Duke asked.

The neighbour nodded. "You've not listened to the forecast then?"

He shook his head.

"There's quite a big one approaching, but nothing will keep Luca from getting out in it. Shows in her paintings too."

THE GATEWAY TO HELL

Mia climbed up the greasy stairs and shone the torch at the trap door, studying it from every angle. She pushed it, but it was firmly and solidly fixed in place, nothing was about to shift it.

"It's no good," she said, elbowing it angrily. "It won't budge. But we don't want to be here when they open that trap door again."

She flopped down next to Hani and rubbed her forehead, trying to keep the fear from her voice when she next spoke. "We just need to keep calm."

Hani looked at her. "I think we might have reached the end of the road…"

"No, the Duke will help us."

"Then why hasn't he come back to find us yet?"

She felt a terrible icy fear creep from her feet upwards at these words. She couldn't bear it, the thought of having to wait here for their fate; a helpless captive. Had they both been abandoned and betrayed yet again by another adult they trusted?

It felt damp and gloomy and cold down here, like being buried alive. For a moment she remembered the house in Grangefield with sudden affection, wishing she was back there now, in her room, having nothing more to worry about than a load of school bullies who persisted in making her daily life miserable. Even that seemed preferable to this...

Even Angie and Clifford with their widescreen TV and their plans for an extension, and their attempts to sound sincere and feign an interest in her school life.

Even that...

"What are you thinking about?"

Hani's words broke into her thoughts.

She shook her head. "I was just remembering my foster parents."

Hani waited, listening.

"I hated it, but I'd give anything to be back there now."

"You have me to blame for that," Hani said.

"No. I ran away."

"You didn't have to help me."

"Yes, I did. Without you I wouldn't have got very far at all. I'd have been lonely."

He gave a small ironic laugh, looking around the dark cellar. "And are you lonely now?"

"It's so damp in here," she murmured after a while.

She shone the torch onto the floor where more puddles were slowly forming. The ground was wet, and if anything, it seemed to be getting wetter.

"We're near the sea, the tide could be rising."

"But inside?"

They clambered onto an empty crate in the corner to keep dry, and watched the tide creep slowly higher.

Hani was seized by panic and fear. "It's rising."

Mia did not speak, for the same thought had occurred to her. *What if the cellar floods at high tide?*

She jumped down from the crate and splashed across to the other side.

"It must be coming in from somewhere," she said breathlessly, moving around in the dark. "And if it's coming in, then maybe we can get out the same way."

Hani watched her in silence, his terror of water taking hold of him again.

Mia shone the torch into the far corner, pulled a crate aside, and gasped at what she saw. She had revealed a round low entrance, like a sewer, through which the tidal water was seeping.

"Here. Look." She shone the torch over it. "Maybe we can escape this way."

Hani jumped down from the crate, ankle-deep in water, and looked at where she pointed the torch. It gaped like the gateway to hell.

"No."

He backed away. "I can't go in there."

"It's our only chance," Mia said. "We haven't got much time. If we go now, then maybe we can beat the tide before it rises."

"I don't like that word – maybe!"

Again, he shook his head, and she could feel the terror coming off him in waves, as flashbacks to the horrors of his sea journey flooded his mind.

"What if we get stuck or trapped?" he added, imagining a gate or grill at the end of the tunnel. "What if we drown?"

Mia looked back at him in the dark and said the only thing that came into her head. "What if we stay here?"

Suddenly, from above, there was another loud burst of movement, shouting and then laughter.

193

Hani moved closer to Mia and stepped towards the entrance of the low tunnel.

"We need to crawl," she said.

"Wait," he took the purple silk scarf and knotted it around his head. "Now we can go."

Then he followed her into the mouth of hell.

RACE AGAINST THE TIDE

Pure terror was what Hani felt as he followed behind his friend, splashing through   freezing sea water on his hands and knees.

Mia was talking to him all the time, trying to reassure him in her own way. "This isn't too bad, actually. I'm sure I could join the army, you know. I'd easily manage military training. It takes your mind off the hunger anyway." And then, "I could murder a hot dog just now. Do you get hot dogs in Syria?"

Hani found himself smirking. She was chattering away, pointlessly, endlessly, trying to take his mind off things.

"All that training in the stadium did some good, you know. Ugh! What's that? Don't panic – it's nothing. Nothing at all to worry about… take it nice and easy."

She did not voice her own fears. She did not admit that she too was terrified they would not be able to beat the tide; she could feel it rising higher, steadily climbing the walls. She instinctively knew how badly Hani needed someone to calm him, to give him courage, so she kept on talking, on and on, because she could not use the flashlight, and she did not want to stop. She also dreaded what Hani had hinted at, that perhaps they would run up against a grill or gate of some kind, and then they would be trapped, and they would drown in this eerie darkness, and no one would know and no one would find them.

She closed her mind to her thoughts, tried to stem the flow of panic, and concentrated instead on breathing deeply, putting all her efforts into reassuring Hani with light-hearted banal chatter and making sure they kept on moving.

How *long* the tunnel seemed, an underground passage which no one ever used, a sewer-like construction which flooded the cellar of *Balfour House* at high tide.

She heard a sound behind her. A moan.

"I can't do this," Hani said, his voice breaking.

"Yes! Yes, you can. Think of Reena. Think of the hot dogs. If we get to the end of this tunnel you can find her. We can find her. We can…"

"But it's rising more quickly."

He was right.

They could sense the waves pounding on the shore beyond, and the sea level was creeping higher, as high as their bellies, so they were having to push their way forward, their faces getting wet, and the terror was uncontrollable, especially for Hani – as memories of his sea voyage came flooding back.

Then Mia heard him behind her, weeping, and he was ashamed to be crying because he had always promised Reena he would be brave, and now here he was, frightened and at the end of his tether.

He wondered how ironic it would be if he drowned here, his face submerged beneath the water level of the tunnel, having survived the storms and high seas of the Mediterranean.

Suddenly Mia stopped. She could see a light up ahead, faintly glowing, a sign the end was in sight.

"We've made it, Hani," she cried. "It's the end of the tunnel."

She crawled out first onto the rocks, then bent to help him. They clung to each other as they clambered to their feet, buffeted by waves as they splashed against the shore.

The sea was wild, crashing inland.

Another two minutes and they would have been completely submerged, trapped in the cellar as the tide swept in below the foundations of *Balfour House*.

They held each other in the gathering dark, listening to the waves crash, feeling the cold air on their faces, then scrambled across the rocks to a higher spot. The sea had covered most of the beach.

They were still not far from *Balfour House*. It rose above them eerily in the stormy gloom, its dirty-yellow walls concealing secrets, its high windows giving nothing away. But inside that building were men who wanted to hurt them.

Hani clutched Mia's hand and together they stumbled away from the shore, the wind whipping their faces.

When he looked back, he could see dark clouds gathering over the sea. "It looks as if a storm's on its way."

"We don't want to be near this place when they discover we're missing," she shouted back against the wind.

"Maybe they'll just leave us there for dead."

They scrambled their way up the steep bank, away from the pounding surf and onto the tarmac road. Just as they reached it they heard the sky rumble far out to sea.

They stood and looked back. Flashes of white lightening rippled and quivered in the distance, striking the surface of the waves. A curtain of stormy rain was sweeping the coastline, heading towards them.

Where was the Duke?

Why had he not come back to find them?

Could they trust him, or had he betrayed them like everyone else?

They turned and glimpsed a light in an upstairs window of *Balfour House*, a figure passing in front of it. The figure lifted a flashlight and seemed to be pointing it out across the waves, as if they were signalling to someone.

In the darkness, Hani watched. Far out to sea was the boat he'd seen earlier, a small white yacht of some kind and it was being tossed about helplessly on the waves. Was this who the men were signalling to?

Why?

The thought crossed both their minds at the same time. Maybe Reena was on that yacht. But if so, how would they ever reach her?

A STORM

A light shone out to sea, as the boat bobbed about furiously on the waves.

"It's signalling back. Look," Hani said.

But Mia's attention was fixed on the house, where she had seen someone emerge around the corner of the gable end. There was movement there; something was happening.

She pulled Hani by the arm and they lay flat on their stomachs in a hollow, fitting their bodies to the turf, peering through the marram grass.

There were shouts from the house, a commotion, and they could see Yusuf standing outside, gesturing with his arms at one of the other men. Uncle Giorgio was nowhere in sight.

Had their absence been discovered?

Then Uncle Giorgio reappeared and joined Karl and it soon became clear they were heading down to the beach.

Yusuf, however, climbed into the black jeep, parked on the verge, and began to reverse it.

"Come on," Mia nudged Hani, who tore his gaze away, and they began to crawl their way along in the dark. They could hear the sea driving against the rocks, the wind whipping up. Gathering rain clouds obscured the moon.

Once *Balfour House* was out of sight they began to run. It felt as if they were racing the approaching storm.

Hani turned to look back at the sea, seeking out the white speck of the boat lost in the void of churning water and brooding storm clouds out in the bay. If Reena was out on that boat, how terrified would she be? It would remind her of what they had been through, trying to get to Europe in the first place, the terrible journey they'd been lucky enough to survive while others perished.

The sky cracked overhead and the rain caught up with them. The wind was howling like a banshee as it tore through the dark air. They could barely see ahead now, but kept running in the darkness, their faces wet, heading towards the distant lights of the village.

"We need to find the Duke," Mia said.

Neither of them wanted to voice their fear – that he had betrayed them, like everyone else. They had to believe in him still.

Another thought occurred to Mia. If the Duke, in his desperation, had turned to the police for help, Mia would be 'found' and returned to Angie and Clifford like lost property.

She didn't want that, but perhaps it was a sacrifice she would have to make in the end, for Hani's sake and for the sake of his sister, Reena – if she was still alive.

Hani had to know what had happened to his sister otherwise he would never stop looking for her. That was what happened when a person went missing, Mia knew that. The relatives of the loved-one never ceased to hope, and kept on searching for the rest of their lives.

How many refugee children had been lost, never to be found again?

Mia was technically a Missing Person, but she did not believe that Angie and Clifford would keep looking for *her*. They would forget. She was not irreplaceable. She was a foster child: in care. And foster children come and go – everyone knows that. As easily replaced as a stray dog.

But if she had to be returned to them for the sake of Hani and his sister, then she would submit to that fate, until she found the next opportunity to run...

When they saw a pair of headlights on the road above them they feared the worst. For one wonderful moment they hoped it was the Duke in his battered old Land Rover, but instead the familiar black jeep they knew so well hove into view.

To their left they could see a steep path beginning at the edge of the cliff and winding down treacherously to the dark shoreline below. They began to head towards it, and down the slope to avoid being seen from above. Wooden steps had been carved into the side of the rock face, twisting down to a massive inlet or natural harbour, cut into the rocks by the pressure of the tide, where the sea boomed in a terrifying cauldron of sound.

They had not dared to use the flashlight, so it was possible they had not yet been seen from the road by the driver of that lone vehicle. It was too dark, surely? And the windscreen of the vehicle would be misted with the downpour.

Mia and Hani were both drenched, and the wind howled all around them. They held fast to the path, terrified of being blown off balance.

When they were a few metres down they glanced back up the side of the cliff.

"He'll have driven past," Mia said. "He won't have seen us."

Yusuf peered above the steering wheel, through the driving rain, leaning forward, the wipers on full. The storm was pushing and buffeting against the sides of the jeep like a wild animal, and he could barely see the road ahead of him.

He had gone out alone, looking for the prisoners who had escaped yet again. The others had stayed behind, searching the beach and the shoreline. Yusuf preferred to seek out their quarry alone. He had a sixth sense for this kind of thing.

He rounded the headland and for the first time began to doubt they could have got this far. Not in these conditions, with a storm raging, and the rain sleeting inland.

He stopped the vehicle in a tourist lay-by, and gazed over the cliff face.

His headlights picked out a large information board on the edge of the cliff.

Smoo Cave. The largest sea cave in Britain, with inner chambers going far beneath the land's surface, only accessible by boat as they were filled with dark lakes of icy sea water, deep and still.

Yusuf switched off his engine and killed the headlights. Darkness, with the wind pushing against the vehicle.

He edged the door open with difficulty, struggling against the force of the storm as it threatened to whip the car door from its hinges. He bent his head and ran towards the edge of the cliff.

The sea boomed below him. It was a wild night and about to get much wilder.

He couldn't make out the young people at first. There was no sign of them. Perhaps they'd kept to the road ahead?

Then Yusuf noticed the wooden steps carved into the side of the rock, a dangerous cliff path twisting down to the cave entrance hundreds of feet below.

SMOO CAVE

"What is this place?" Mia wondered out loud.

Neither of them knew that it was called *Smoo Cave*, and it was the largest sea cave in Britain. All *they* knew was that they had descended a cliff, with the help of a set of wooden steps, and now they were hanging perilously against the side of the rocks. Below them were a couple of crumbling ruins, evidence of a fishing settlement; abandoned houses where people had once lived and eked out a living from the sea, even using the vast cathedral-like entrance of the cave itself as a shelter and workshop.

Now it was left to the elements, visited only by sea birds and seals in winter, tourists in the summer.

Hani raised his head and glanced up the side of the cliff. Above, he spotted a familiar dark figure, silhouetted against the sky, peering down at them.

His heart lurched into his mouth.

They had been seen.

Yusuf licked his lips and wiped the rain from his forehead.

It was sheeting against the coastline while the wind roared and as he peered over the edge of the cliff, he saw the glint of a torch and two pale faces peering back up at him.

Yusuf cursed himself, wishing now he had not come out alone. He was beginning to get a handle on these kids; over the past few days he'd become increasingly aware of their doggedness and determination, and part of him could not help feeling a reluctant admiration. They were resourceful, it was true, but he was a wolf and he would hunt them down.

He would not pause or hesitate.

Uncle Giorgio had entrusted him with this task and he would keep going because he had his own reasons for doing so.

Those reasons hovered at the back of his mind now, but he pushed them relentlessly down.

He bent his head, concentrating on his footfall, and proceeded to make his way down the steep and precipitous cliff path.

"It looks dangerous down there," Hani said, clinging to the side of the cliff as they edged their way down.

"We've got no choice."

The wind screamed in their ears and the rain tore at the cliff face, but they put their heads down and concentrated on their footing. They were conscious all the time of Yusuf behind them, following the twists and turns, in pursuit even when he was out of sight. They had to slow their pace to negotiate the steeper parts of the path until they reached the bottom of the cliff. What they would do once they were down there hadn't occurred to them yet, but they had no other option.

The ruin of a small crofter's cottage clung to a buttress of rock near the cave entrance, its stones scattered on the rocky shore, its walls still intact. It was more sheltered from the wind here, although the tide was higher than it ought to be.

Hani glanced behind, but he could no longer see the dark figure of Yusuf.

They kept on going, down into the cave entrance which towered above them, high and eerie like a stone cathedral, echoing and rumbling with the sound of the distant waves.

Around them the cave walls dripped. Suddenly the roar of wind and sea was reduced to a distant murmur and they could hear its echo reverberating at the back of the cave.

Mia did not turn the flashlight on this time, but peered into the darkness. Could they wait for him to come down and then double back on him? But it was too late for that.

They could see the beam of an iPhone flashlight wavering over the wet rocks, probing like the snout of a hunting creature.

They dropped back into the shadows, feeling their way in the dark.

Taking refuge behind a thick ledge of stone they waited, keeping their heads low.

The sea rumbled in the distance, waves hitting the shore but not quite reaching the cave itself, breaking a few yards from the entrance.

They heard his footsteps, saw the gleam of his phone exploring the floor of the cave, the ceiling and the walls.

He was lifting the beam higher, revealing its height, as if he might find them there. Huge buttresses supported a hollow dome of rock, towering above them like a man-made cathedral.

At last Yusuf shouted out to them, "I know you're in here."

There was a deathly silence, filled only with the muted sounds of the wind.

"You may as well come out now. You know we will find you."

Mia laid a reassuring hand on Hani's arm. "He's on his own," she whispered.

"I admire you, in a way, yes I do..." his voice echoed against the black rock. "Very resourceful. But you cannot keep on like this forever. You know that now."

While he spoke, Mia saw a dark shape lying crosswise on the rocks behind them. She felt around it. A small rubber dinghy was pulled up on the rocks.

She nudged Hani and together they crept and slid around it. It was pulled up inches from a deep-water channel, leading into the first great underground chamber, accessible only by boat.

It usually sat in the water, waiting for tourists, but this early in the year there were none, particularly not at night, during a storm.

They waited until they heard Yusuf's footsteps grow distant, retreating to the far side of the cave, his phone flashlight rippling across the walls, seeking out the crevices and corners. Then he suddenly swiped it off and stood still, plunging the cave into blackness. Trying to catch them out.

Mia and Hani used the opportunity to step quietly around the dinghy, then they grabbed a hold of it, dragged it across the few inches of rock, and let it fall into the water, dropping down after it.

The small raft rocked with the impact. There was a moment of panic as Mia wondered if they had left the oars behind, but she discovered them lying prone in the bottom of the boat, so she lifted an oar, wedged it against the rock, and pushed off into the deep dark water. In the same instant Yusuf flicked his flashlight back on and raced towards them... but too late.

They had forced the dinghy forward through the narrow channel of rock into the first chamber, a pool of fathomless black water beneath them. Yusuf could only stand by helpless as they forced their way forward.

UNDERGROUND LAKES

Yusuf stood on the side of the wooden platform, watching as the rubber dinghy moved further away from him, with Hani and Mia on board.

The flashlight on his phone threw out one feeble beam of light into the surrounding dark, which glinted against the inky-black water. He stood with his fists clenched in frustration.

He was letting them get away.

But get away, to where?

They would be lost in those underground chambers. Trapped, with only one way to get out, and that was the way they had come in.

He could wait here for them to return but he needed to contact the others – Uncle Giorgio and Karl, and there was no way he could get a mobile signal through the fathoms of rock above his head.

He had a choice.

He could return to *Balfour House* to fetch the others or he could wait here in the darkness, hoping that Hani and the girl would panic and make their way back.

How long would his phone battery last?

How long before Uncle Giorgio and Karl came looking for him?

Mia clicked their own small flashlight on, and it lit up only a tiny part of the surrounding darkness. The danger was immense, and the challenges greater. They could hear Yusuf shouting behind them, but his words were lost.

They rowed their way steadily to a channel ahead of them which took them into a second chamber. The darkness appeared to deepen perceptibly and then it lightened again. They could hear the sound of a waterfall. Then they saw it. It was pouring in a torrent through a sinkhole in the cliff-top high above them and although the sky was darkened with storm clouds, a silvery light filtered down into the cave along with the waterfall. They felt its spray on their faces and were careful to steer away from it for fear of being caught and the boat capsized.

The network of tunnels stretched before them, reaching out fingers of watery darkness through the black earth. How deep could they go without getting lost?

Hani dipped the oars and listened to the gentle pull. The water was deep and black and fathomless. Mia had flicked the flashlight off to save the battery. The roof of the chamber echoed above them, soaring to a great height.

"If we go back now, they'll be waiting for us," Hani said.

"Then what can we do?"
He did not answer.

Yusuf stood alone in the first cave. He couldn't swim. He stared at the point where the boat had disappeared, his iPhone flashlight tracking the surface of the water.

There was nothing he could do.

He could not go after them.

He tried to call Uncle Giorgio, but there was no reception from here, as he had expected.

He waited.

Hani and the girl would have to come out eventually. Or they would die in there, lost in the network of underground tunnels and chambers.

He lifted the flashlight higher and explored the extent of the second water-filled chamber through which their dinghy had drifted. It was truly immense and he could feel the weight of the rock bearing down on him. He thought how foolish it was of them to choose to disappear into the bowels of the earth like that, but he could not blame them.

He thought of the boy Hani, and what had happened to his sister. He remembered them briefly from the carrot-topping shed, how they had worked side by side, how she protected him. Who would have thought the boy would have been so persistent in his pursuit of her? He seemed determined not to give up – such loyalty – and for a long painful moment Yusuf remembered his own sister, a long time ago, in another lifetime, when things had been so different to what they were now, before he had begun to do bad things. Gradually, over the years, his conscience had hardened until only a flicker of remorse remained at any of the actions he took. He didn't usually spare a thought for his victims, the people who came and went. It was a livelihood, a way of surviving, one he had been forced into. If life hadn't been so tough for him when he was young, then maybe he could have avoided all of this, but once caught up in the world of Uncle Giorgio, he had not been able to escape, and the only way forward had been to continue along the same path.

But he too had once had a sister. A long time ago. So long ago, he had almost forgotten. Not because of how many years had passed but because of what those years had been filled with. Crime, revenge, anger and guilt.

He did not usually stop to consider any of this. But something about the terrible, mad persistence of these two children had forced him to now.

That companion of the boy's, who had rescued him at the petrol station... A skinny girl, quick on her feet. She had never met the boy before, as far as Yusuf knew, and yet she had stayed with him all this time, through everything.

And now they were here, lost in the bowels of the earth aboard a small rubber craft, seemingly unaware of the dangers ahead, while a violent storm raged in the sky above.

What did they think this was? he wondered. *Some adventure in a theme park, an underground cave with water rides?*

They were foolish, more stupid than he'd given them credit for, and he was angry with them.

Now he would have to go back and tell Uncle Giorgio that he had lost them. Either that, or he would have to sit here and wait, while the sea boomed and shuddered in the distance. It was not a very appealing prospect, but neither was the thought of returning to *Balfour House* empty-handed. He allowed his flashlight to track the surface of the water where their boat had disappeared. A glistening trail led the way into the darkness.

The silence of the caves was overwhelming. It was like being buried under the earth, so much rock above them... the weight of the land itself. Mia felt dizzy with it.

She listened again to the gentle plash of their oars in the black water.

"We should stop a while," she said.

"Why?"

Mia clicked the torch on again and shone it around the chamber.

"We don't want to get lost," she whispered. Her words echoed back at them from the walls... hissing the word *lost, lost, lost...*

"We came through *that* tunnel," Hani said, taking the flashlight from her and pointing its beam towards one of the openings.

"How do you know?"

He didn't reply.

"How long do you think he'll wait?" Mia asked.

She didn't expect Hani to answer her. What could he say? She was merely thinking out loud.

They slipped their oars for a moment and drifted, listening for any sound beyond the tunnel.

Would he fetch the others and come after them? How difficult would that be?

It was claustrophobic, being down here, fathoms of rock and earth above their heads.

It made them feel very small.

The world was such a dark, cold hostile place, with so little kindness in it. They were pitted against the elements, had nowhere else to go, and no one to save them. Not even the Duke, it seemed.

YUSUF

Below the earth, Hani and Mia could hear nothing at first of the storm which raged above. The silence was all-encompassing, punctuated by the drip of the cave walls, and the gentle slap of their oars in the water.

After a while an odd sound began to penetrate, like the indrawn breath of a distant monster – that's what it sounded like – as the storm outside built apace.

Then they heard a more ominous sound coming from the chamber they'd just left. It was the low persistent buzz of an engine, and it was heading their way.

Mia and Hani exchanged glances, then began to frantically steer the boat into the shelter of an overhanging alcove. Hani clicked off the torch, plunging them back into darkness.

The waspish hum of the engine grew louder, closer, as a small rubber dinghy with an outboard motor appeared in the archway, its cone of light going before it. It came on towards them, heading in their direction.

They remained in darkness, moored against the side of the chamber, their palms touching the overhang of wet rock above their heads, hoping for the best.

Had Yusuf managed to contact the others so quickly, and had they been able to join him here? No, he must have located another boat in the cave, one with an engine.

They waited.

The motor boat passed them on the far side of the water-filled chamber, and from the look of it there was only one individual on board. Yusuf was alone.

He killed the engine and looked about, projecting the searchlight of his iPhone into the far corners. Mia and Hani held their breath, clinging close to the cave walls, trying to avoid moving or causing the water to stir.

Then they watched as he restarted the engine and proceeded on under the next archway.

Quickly and silently Hani manipulated the oars and handed one to Mia. Then they manoeuvred their boat out into the open, smoothly paddling their way back, in the opposite direction to Yusuf. Hopefully the hum of his own engine would obscure the sound of their movements.

The tension between them was palpable. They were swift and silent, barely speaking, Hani holding the torch in his mouth and shining it ahead to light their way, the darkness pressing down on all sides.

They got through the next chamber, and were just entering the one with the waterfall pouring down from the sinkhole above. If they were quick, they could make it to the first cave, and back out into the night, but Yusuf was quicker.

They heard that persistent waspish drone and he was there, behind them, gaining on them, his searchlight finding them in the darkness.

They pulled at their oars frantically, but they were no match for a motor-powered boat.

He pulled up alongside them and made as if to grab the side of their raft.

Hani dropped the torch, raised his oar, and pushed him away.

"Wait," Yusuf said. "It is dangerous here. The storm is getting worse, and that means these caves will no longer be safe. There isn't much time."

Mia thought for a moment of the strange sound they'd heard earlier, like the indrawn breath of a monster. She hesitated.

"If you keep going, you will be lost. There is no other way out of here, and Uncle Giorgio... he is coming for you."

Hani's eyes narrowed with fury. "Where is my sister? What have you done to her?"

"Your sister is safe," Yusuf cried. "And if you come with me, you will see."

There was a silence.

"Why should I believe you?"

"No reason," Yusuf said. "I admit there is no reason why you should believe me. Other than the fact you have no choice."

"We do have a choice," Hani shouted, and he pushed Yusuf's boat away so hard that Yusuf himself lost his balance.

They watched in silence as he seemed to fall in slow motion, his arms waving before he hit the water. It was the terror on his face which alerted them to the fact he could not swim.

He splashed helplessly in the water, while Hani and Mia watched.

They saw his face sink below the surface of the black

lake then he rose again, his arms flailing. He sank again before rising one more time and they found themselves silently asking the question…Could they let him drown? And watch while he did so?

Mia glanced at her friend, and saw him wrestling with his own emotions. She saw anger and hate and rage there, but she also saw something else…

Then, quick as a flash, before their enemy could sink for the third and final time, Hani suddenly reached out, leant over the side of the boat and grabbed hold of Yusuf.

Yusuf grasped hold of him and then gripped a rope on the side of the dinghy as Hani hauled him to safety.

Mia watched anxiously, waiting for the moment when Yusuf would plunge Hani into the water in his place. Hani could swim, she knew that, but still she waited…

Instead Yusuf sat heavily in the boat, shivering and wiping the water from his eyes. He coughed and spluttered then spoke. "Thank you."

Hani stared in shocked silence: Mia too. And still they did not trust him.

"You saved my life. I cannot swim."

Hani was speechless. He did not know what to say to this devious man who had pursued them halfway across Scotland, who had helped to kidnap his sister, and watched he and Reena – and others like them – while they slaved away in the miserable sheds of the factory farm.

And now he was thanking him for saving his life?

Yusuf couldn't meet Hani's eye, but glanced away.

Then he gestured with his head towards the entrance.

"We'd better go. We have to beat the tide. I meant what I said. Uncle Giorgio is on his way."

"And you think we'll help you?" Hani asked.

Yusuf shook his head. "No, but if we make it out of the cave before he arrives…" he shrugged, "then maybe you will be able to continue on your journey."

Hani stared at him, shaking with fury. "Our *journey* was to find my sister. I go nowhere without her."

Yusuf shrugged again. "Then maybe you have wasted your time."

Mia studied Hani's face as they waited for Yusuf's next words.

"She is gone. You are too late."

"You said she was safe!" Hani choked.

"I lied."

Hani pulled back the oar in readiness to propel it forwards and knock Yusuf out of the boat, but Mia stopped him.

"She is safe," Mia said, "that's what you said, isn't it?"

Yusuf wiped his brow.

"The truth is, I don't know."

He scratched his head. "Maybe she is safe, maybe she is not. But we need to move. We cannot stay here. The storm is building outside and I do not reckon these caves will be so safe then."

Even as he spoke they could hear a distant boom and groan from above, as if the earth was alive and waking from a long slumber.

"He's right," Mia said. "If the sea rises, it could flood these tunnels."

Hani was silent, still nursing his rage.

Yusuf sat hunched in the stern, watching them, a defeated and humiliated expression on his face. He appeared to be wrapped in his own thoughts, memories which were difficult to reach. Eventually he spoke. "You know, I had a sister once – like you."

Hani stared at him in surprise, wondering why Yusuf was telling him this.

Yusuf met his gaze and didn't look away this time. It was as if he was remembering something long forgotten, something he had chosen to bury in the past.

"She was murdered." That was all he said. He didn't bother to explain or elaborate and they did not ask him.

They began to row past an archway of stone, natural pillars supporting the rock above. Hani looked at Yusuf and swallowed back his resentment. "Who murdered her?"

"People. On the other side of a conflict. Americans, actually. They bombed our village. There was a wedding. We were children at the time. She was three years younger than me. There were many buildings destroyed. We did not find her body."

Hani lowered his oar into the black water and pulled at the current. They passed the sinkhole through which the waterfall poured and then out into the first chamber where they'd found the boats.

They heard the roar of the sea long before they emerged. It echoed and boomed in the distance. The shudder and groan of the cave walls made them glance at each other fearfully.

Mia and Hani were suddenly terrified they had been fooled by Yusuf, that they would find Uncle Giorgio waiting for them outside with reinforcements and they would have no time to escape.

But Uncle Giorgio was not the only threat facing

them that night. The sea had risen and turned the large cave entrance into a churning cauldron. Waves pounded the buttresses of rock, and when they reached the first archway they were almost too late. They had to duck their heads to negotiate the boat through the narrow gap.

Hani felt his terror of the sea returning, memories of being onboard the overcrowded raft as it rode the high waves towards an uncertain future. Back then he had had Reena by his side, but he had watched people drown. He had seen grown men vomiting with fear, and he had seen bodies washed up on the shore, refugees – like him – escaping from war-torn cities, but less fortunate than Hani. They had died on the way. He had seen sights he would never forget. Children lying completely still on the beach, their faces covered in sand, limp and lifeless. Children younger than himself.

He and Reena had clung together, crying as they hit the shore and jumped out onto land, splashing through the shallow waves, sobbing with fear and sorrow. Parents had clung to small children, husbands to wives, but most were alone. Solitary passengers who had risked the journey to freedom because they were strong enough and young enough to do so.

Hani remembered how it felt to put his feet on dry land. It had moved and rocked beneath him as if he was still out at sea.

He could remember how the people on board had wept with longing and terror from the moment they first caught sight of land in the distance. They had headed to that distant shore, their gazes fixed upon it, and watched as other boats, small inadequate rafts like their own, did not make it.

The nearer they got to that strip of land, the further it seemed to retreat. The dread, the panic was palpable, the longing painful.

He would never forget.

And now, faced with the rising tide and the spray hitting the rocks in the cave entrance, he knew that the sea had come to claim him after all, like a hungry beast cheated of its prey, returning, unsatisfied, for more.

A BOAT IN DISTRESS

Above *Smoo Cave* the night was turning wild. An Atlantic storm swept in off the ocean, and the White Star yacht moored out in the bay was joined by other forces. There were helicopters sweeping the sky, despite the appalling conditions, their searchlights scanning the grey waves in search of survivors.

Residents in Balnakeil Craft Village had seen the boat in distress and called the local coastguard, who had put out a Mayday.

One of those local residents was Luca Toft, an artist who had come to live in the Craft Village thirty years ago from Iceland.

On nights like this, when a storm threatened to engulf the entire coastline, she did not keep to her little room with its lit stove, she went out with her field glasses to investigate. She was dressed in waterproofs from head to toe and listened to them whisper as she strolled into the night. She was eccentric, she knew, but in this village everyone was eccentric and she was allowed to do whatever she wanted. If she wanted to stroll out into the middle of a storm in her waterproofs then she could, so long as she made sure she was safe.

She stood on a high knoll and watched as lights

signalled to each other, back and forth, across the bay – from *Balfour House* which was supposed to be empty and abandoned – to a small yacht moored out to sea.

The air swirled with energy and there was movement and frenzy everywhere... in just the same manner that Luca tried to capture in her paintings. Movement was the key. But her interest was caught by the yacht in the bay. She peered through her field glasses and although it was almost impossible to see in the dark, the light from the stern of the boat shone briefly on white figures in the water. Her breath stopped in her throat.

She lifted the field glasses again and tried to focus more clearly.

There... she found the point of movement again. One or two figures lost in the sea.

She turned and ran back to the village, the grass whipping her ankles and the rain sheeting down.

A CHANGE OF HEART

The roar was deafening in the cave. It was clear that the long inlet of this natural harbour was about to be breached.

Mia and Hani abandoned the boat and scrambled to the safety of the higher rocks, near where the ruined croft sat. Yusuf followed close behind.

Wind and rain whipped their faces. They stood and looked back at Smoo Cave as it began to fill, their backs up against the broken walls of the ruined croft house. One of the stones above them toppled from the ruin and landed at their feet, beside others. This croft house had withstood these elements for two hundred years or more since its owners had fled. How many storms had lashed this roofless structure, and how many more would it take before all the stones lay scattered in the sparse grasses which clung to the cliffside?

All three turned to scramble towards the cliff path.

They were so drenched it was exhausting trying to pull themselves up. They laboured on, the wind whistling past their ears and threatening to knock them off-balance.

The cliffside offered them some form of temporary shelter, but when they got to the top, the force of the gale increased, hitting them full in the face. Their words were snatched away when they tried to speak, leaving them breathless.

Yusuf was shouting at them.

"What?"

"You can go on now, from here," he was yelling. "I will say nothing."

Hani stared at Yusuf in disbelief. "I don't believe you."

Yusuf shrugged again. Then he shouted back so that Hani could hear.

"You can believe what you like."

"But Uncle Giorgio… he will know…"

"Then I will pay the price, if he does. But I doubt it."

When Hani still did not believe him, Yusuf shouted, "We are the same. You and I."

Hani glared at him angrily and shook his head. "I will never be the same as you."

Yusuf shrugged again then shouted back "I hope not. I was once like you are now. A boy in trouble. And now I am a man…" His words trailed off as if he had nothing more to say. It was in the stars; it was fated, he seemed to be saying, and there was nothing he could do about any of it now.

Hani was confused. He could not understand how this man could have undergone such a seismic change, and he did not trust it. Had Yusuf simply lost the appetite for a fight? Hani would never accept that they were the same.

Hani would never be capable of such acts of cruelty no matter how much he suffered in life. He would never resort to the kind of life Yusuf had chosen.

"People have a choice," Hani shouted. "They always have a choice."

Yusuf wasn't interested. "Now," he yelled. "You go."

But before they could act on his words Mia grabbed hold of Hani's arm and pointed. "Look."

She had seen the lights out on the bay. A chopper flying low, buffeted by the storm, a coastguard crew on a second boat alongside the yacht they had spied earlier, struggling against the waves.

Hani stared in horror. "My sister is on that boat..." but his words were spoken so quietly they were lost on the wind.

RESCUE ATTEMPT

By the time Hani and Mia reached the shore a small crowd had gathered in the darkness before the looming edifice of *Balfour House*.

The coastguard, the police, the Duke, Luca Toft and other locals from the nearby Balnakeil Craft Village were scattered about, either helping or witnessing events unfold. A flashing blue light bathed the side of the house, from the emergency vehicles parked above the beach on the road.

Of Uncle Giorgio, Karl and even Yusuf there was no sign. They had melted into the darkness before the police arrived.

Mia stood in the shadows next to Hani.

A heavy-looking policeman bore down on them and shouted, "We don't want spectators."

Mia shrank back, but Hani's gaze was fixed on the rescue attempt out at sea.

"My sister is on board."

"What?"

The police officer turned to stare at him, and the penny seemed to drop.

A coastguard came striding across the dunes, the

wind buffeting his words away. But one word stood out from all the rest.

"Traffickers."

There was a ripple of unease from the onlookers, Luca Toft among them.

"Any survivors?" another asked.

"Wait and see. Hopeful."

The man spoke in short clipped tones.

The Duke stepped forward and laid an arm across each of their shoulders.

Mia looked up at him. "We thought you'd left us!"

He didn't reply. There was no use explaining that he had tried to get help. His thoughts were distracted by what was needed down at the shore and he moved forward to help the men in the lifeboat who were struggling against the pounding waves.

A police constable stopped him. "Excuse me, sir!"

The Duke stood still and watched and Hani came to stand beside him, staring out to sea in the dark, waiting to see what would happen next.

Mia had fallen back into the shadows of the sand dunes where no one could see her, and studied the commotion from a safe distance. She had watched the adults gathered near and decided she couldn't stay beside Hani any longer. She did not want to be seen.

She did not know what the future held for her, but she would not be returned to Grangefield and a life in care. She would not be told by others what to do, where to go... even though the alternative might be filled with risk and danger. Her island was still within reach. She hadn't got there yet, but maybe one day she would, and then she would be able to tell stories of how long it took her to reach it and how many adventures she had had along the way.

She did not want to be separated from Hani either, so she stayed near, watching.

The woman called Luca was bending low and speaking to him. She had an arm across his shoulder and was offering him words of comfort. Mia could see all of this, even as the rain swept the beach and drenched the onlookers.

Suddenly Mia felt more like an outsider than ever. She wondered if she was about to lose her only friend.

As she watched the people enfold him, caring for him, she felt like an outcast. Since the day her parents and her grandmother had died, leaving her an orphan, she had been set adrift in life... singled out to be unlucky. That's what being *in care* meant. It meant the opposite of being *cared for*. It had always struck Mia as ironic that the authorities used this expression to describe herself and others like her. *Looked after*. It was what they wrote on the forms. She had seen it written there on her own case files.

And yet, *looked after* was not how she felt at all.

Once again, she had landed on all the squares with the snakes.

She crouched low and listened to the wind screaming through the marram grass that whipped her face. She felt close to the earth. The grasses, the sand dunes, the reeds... she was a part of all these things. Not people. It was not people she wanted to be near right now.

People hurt you.

People let you down.

She listened to the elements roaring and stayed quietly in the shadows to see what would happen next.

When the crowd parted, she caught a glimpse of a sight that would stay with her forever. The lights from the coastguard picked out a scene that looked like one of the images in the Children's Bible her gran used to own: people's faces, awed in exclamation, their eyes wide, bathed in yellow radiance, while at the centre stood Hani and another figure – a young woman with long dark hair, whose arms were wrapped around the little brother she had promised always to protect.

Reena had survived. She hadn't perished in the water or at the hands of Uncle Giorgio and his men.

Hani was reunited with his sister.

Mia wiped the rainwater from her eyes to check she was not imagining any of it.

They held each other, crying, and adults stood by, wondering what to do, what to make of it all; figures stepped forward and wrapped the girl in sheets of what looked like silver foil.

As if they were going to bake her in the oven for Christmas dinner, Mia thought.

She was pleased for Hani.

Then she saw him turn and look about the beach, his eyes searching the darkness, searching for his friend. The crowd closed around him, but he pushed them aside briefly, still searching.

Mia wavered about what to do next.

Her friend Hani was surrounded by adults, figures of authority who complied with and followed the letter of the law, who would take control of Mia's future and persuade themselves that they were acting in her best interests.

She felt painfully torn.

She longed to step out of the darkness, run across the storm-lashed beach and join him, wrap her arms about him and tell him how pleased she was he had found his sister after all... but something made her stay where she was.

She couldn't run out to join him.

She retreated further into the shadows, feeling her heart ache. Never had she felt so lonely in all her life.

The woman called Luca Toft noticed Hani's distress and followed his gaze. She wrinkled her brow and frowned out into the darkness, but of Mia she could see no sign.

The small skinny girl with the wings on her ankles had already fled.

She was running away from the adults... and she would keep running.

TO THE ISLAND...

Suddenly, out of the darkness loomed a figure, stopping her in her tracks.

"And where do you think you're going?" a kindly voice spoke, shouting above the wind.

Mia hung her head. "The island?" she suggested.

"Ah, yes, the infamous island."

It was the Duke, and he wrapped a waterproof around her shoulders. "Do you know what I think, Mia?"

She shook her head.

"I think you need to be with Hani right now."

And he led her back to the waiting group, where individuals parted to see Hani turn with relief and pull his new friend into his tight circle.

"This," he was shrieking against the wind, to his sister Reena. "This is Mia. She saved me. And she saved you."

Everyone stared at Mia and for the first time in her short life she felt like the most important person in the world.

"You're not going anywhere," the Duke reminded her gently. "You're staying with us."

And he meant it. "Do you think I'm going to see you children suffer after all you've been through?"

"But Angie and Clifford?" Mia began.

"You don't have to go back to Angie and Clifford. Or to Grangefield. I want all three of you to come and live with me."

"With you?"

The Duke nodded. "In my house. Greystone Hall. And did you know there are schools and academies with vast stadiums where you can learn how to train properly? You can run as fast as you like then, and still no one will catch you. And maybe… just maybe, one day we'll all go to that island of yours. Visit the house where your parents lived."

Mia stared and she stared.

And the waves continued to pound the shore. And when the police officers and constables asked questions, the Duke answered them as if he was the one in command, and no one could argue with him.

"What is this island, Hani?" Reena whispered, looking at her little brother.

He shook his head, unable to speak at first.

One day – he knows – he will tell his sister about it.

The island is a place like no other, he will tell Reena, where people are kind, and life is not cruel. Bullies do not exist, hard men and liars become angels and saints… under the influence of the beautiful sights, the sunsets and sunrises that quite take your breath away, and the endless white beaches.

But part of him knows that they have already found their island of safety.

*

234

They spent the night at Luca Toft's house, and in the morning they drove back in the battered old Land Rover to Greystone Hall: the Duke, Mia, Hani and Reena.

"We will need to think of schooling for you all, but in the holidays you will come here. This place is your home."

And so it began. A new life for them all, far away from the carrot-topping sheds and the glinting polytunnels, far away, also, from the brooding towers of the petrochemical plant, where Angie and Clifford continued to make plans for a new extension to accommodate even more young people into their care.

But Mia was no longer a girl in care.

She was a girl who was loved.

More Alex Nye titles from Fledgling Press:

YA Fiction
Darker Ends

Historical Fiction
For My Sins
Arguing With the Dead

Reviews of *Darker Ends*

"Alex Nye's unadorned prose perfectly captures the chilling feeling of being trapped in a cold and forbidding — yet still beautiful landscape — being watched day and night by a menacing presence."
(*US Review of Books*)

"Each turn of the page leaves you grasping for more."
(*Amazon Customer 5-Star Review*)

"*Darker Ends* is a spooky, atmospheric read that keeps the tension rising right to the very last page."
(*Goodreads*)

"This is a skilled time-slip tale of time, life and consciousness swirled up into a heady brew of mystery and danger."
(*Historical Novel Society*)

"If you are feeling nervous, and would like to read a book to calm you down, I suggest you don't choose Alex Nye's new novel *Darker Ends*."
(*The Bookwitch*)

"A gripping read, suspenseful and atmospheric."
(*Amazon Customer 5-Star Review*)